Sensualities of Time

I0663367

AN ORIGINAL NOVEL

By Bud Seligson

Lost Age Publishing
2017

SENSUALITIES OF TIME © 2016 Bud Seligson

The following original novel has been filed and registered with the Writers' Guild of America, West, under the name of Bud Seligson.

Printed in the United States of America

Cover Art by Cyrusfiction Productions.

ISBN: 978-1-946480-14-9

9018 Balboa Boulevard
Suite #562
Northridge, CA 91325

An adult collection of Bud Seligson's historically correct, very sexy and other interesting short stories and other tid-bits.

DEDICATION PAGE

With the exception of doing the research and touring locations, the life of a writer tends to be very solitary and often boring! Never more so for me, as when I am working under a deadline. Every year, my wife Diane, puts up with the long hours, and the fact, that even when I am home, I am often mentally elsewhere! I am a lucky man to be married to such an awesome and understanding woman.

—Bud Seligson

AN IMPORTANT NOTE FROM BUD SELIGSON

Not many writers actually pay attention to friends, editors and readers when they tell you what they would like to have you write.

Over the past years, I have written many novels, short stories, etc., etc.

I have done so as a ghost writer and as a story writer for other writers.

My many friends and professional writing associates have been 'on my case' lately to put together two of the things that they all tell me that I do best.

It has been suggested many times that for the fun of it, that I should pull out a few of my favorite sexy scenes from several of my historically accurate action stories, and put them into a collection or novel.

I liked the idea and have tried it out within the following novel where each short story is historically accurate and has a steamy and sexual theme to it.

TABLE OF CONTENTS

Sensualities of Time

By Bud Seligson

LEONARDO DA VINCI & MONA LISA

POSSIBLY THE GREATEST LOVE AFFAIR
THE WORLD HAS NEVER KNOWN

§

INTRODUCTION TO LEONARDO DA VINCI

Leonardo da Vinci is the victim of his own celebrity!

The world lines up at the Louvre Museum in Paris for a brief glimpse of the *Mona Lisa*'s cryptic smile. But apart from a few Renaissance scholars, most people are content to honor his genius on the strength of a handful of paintings. This is convenient, admittedly, but unfortunately, it completely overlooks the university of Leonardo's genius. For Leonardo was more than the painter of the *Mona Lisa,* much more.

The man from Vinci also achieved a vast amount in the name of technology and science. He towered head and shoulders above his contemporaries in terms of creativity, in that he was a brilliant engineer, a visionary pioneer, and in many respects, centuries ahead of his own time.

When the Middle Ages gave way to the Renaissance, Florence, Italy, was the center of Europe. It was a Florentine who wrote the first book in the vernacular (in the everyday language of ordinary people in a country or place): *The Divine Comedy.* Florence master builders erected the first massive building dome since the Age of Antiquity; the first nude statue of the Renaissance was created in Florence; the first opera, called *Eurydice,* and the first statistical use for modern banking.

It was a time of flowering for the fine arts and literature, science, philosophy, politics, and religion. The cosmos was no longer something that revolved around the Earth for the edification of mankind. It was a part of the Universe that had to be explored, investigated and examined until it finally revealed its secrets.

The people of Florence were witty, a little cheeky, and always very sure of themselves. This is also a perfect description of our Leonard da Vinci, who was born into this New World with its new attitudes on April 15, 1452. He was born in the city of Vinci, son of the Florentine lawyer Ser Piero and the peasant girl Caterina. He died on May 2, 1519 in the castle at Amboise, France, in the arms of Francis the First, King of France. Leonardo gave his most famous portrait, the *Mona Lisa* to the King, as part of the royal possessions, and the painting that was done by possibly the world's greatest Italian became the property of France, where it has been viewed by millions.

The following is this author's version of how the Mona Lisa came to be painted in his later years by Leonardo. This is the story of the "hot and heavy" love affair as visualized by the author, with all its lust and passion in full view of the reader. This, then, is the story of the love affair between Leonardo da Vinci and Mona Lisa.

§

LEONARDO DA VINCI AND THE SECRET LOVE AFFAIR WITH MONA LISA, THE MOST BEAUTIFUL WOMAN IN THE WORLD. A SHORT AND VERY PASSIONATE LOVE STORY.

Leonardo remembered clearly the first time he saw his Mona Lisa!

He was wandering about the central marketplace of Florence, Italy, enjoying a few days of freedom and simply being on his own with nothing in particular to do. It was great fun being able to stop and sample fresh fruits and other delights from the local vendors. All of these sellers of various items held court within the shadow of the da Vinci castle that loomed far above them all, like a giant protector.

He moved into the grand central square where the last slaves of the day were being offered for sale, and he decided to watch the action for a while. He had never gotten over the strangeness of people actually buying and selling other people!

He did not intend to buy anyone, but he was curious to see just what type of "merchandise" was being offered on the selling block. Slaves from all over the known world were always available to those with the gold or silver to buy them. He saw fair-haired blondes and even wild men from the jungles of deepest Africa.

The bidding was noisy and the buyers, each with their own needs, made offers for strong males to work in their fields or for women to work in their household. These slaves were bought for almost nothing.

The bidders all yelled out their bids loudly and with great hand gestures. Some of the female slaves, several of whom were real beauties, twisted and turned. They were showing off their charms in the hope of attracting a wealthy purchaser who would give them some comforts rather than a cheap hovel that a lowly farmer would provide because he only wanted a slut to slop his pigs and warm his bed at night.

The bidding was brisk, but the prices, as nearly as Leonardo could tell, were reasonable enough for these troubled times. A good-looking wench was going for an average price of nearly two solid gold pieces.

Even though he was standing at the rear of the square, he remembered having no trouble seeing above the heads of the smaller Italians, who were very intent and serious about the bidding. Leonardo knew that gold and silver came and went rapidly through one's fingers in fifteenth-century Florence.

His concern for caution evaporated completely when the auctioneer brought the next offering onto the selling block. He immediately liked what he saw, even though the female slave was filthy, and her hair was hanging down in greasy, tangled tendrils.

Mona, as he later came to call her, was almost completely naked, and it was easy to see that her back showed evidence of a recent lashing. She stood as a caged animal might, twisting and twitching in barely controlled rage. Her head would come to below Leonardo's shoulders, but her breasts were what really attracted him. They were small, though exceedingly well formed and ripe.

The auctioneer made an effort to get her to move around the block, but every movement she made suggested pure hate, which the buyers could easily see, and so the bidding on this she-beast had not started. Holding her face in his hand, the auctioneer pried her mouth open with his rod, showing that her teeth were not as rotten as her disposition. He nearly lost a finger in the doing.

Mona stared out at the would-be buyers with such open hatred that it was scaring all of them off. They wanted a good worker or a willing bed partner, not some bitch who would stick a knife into them the first time they closed their eyes.

Leonardo raised his hand and bid one silver coin.

The auctioneer tried to raise the ante, crying out for another bidder.

There was only silence, and Leonardo thought that he had bought her for this low price, when suddenly, from the opposite side of the square, came another bid of two small gold coins. It was an Arab merchant in a large turban, who must also have had an eye for real beauty.

The bidding between the two of them suddenly became a contest. The woman became secondary now as the two men were really getting into a bidding war. The auctioneer was absolutely loving it as he played one bidder against the other.

When Leonardo locked eyes with the Arab, an instant dislike flared up between them. They each knew that the other would go to the limit of his available wealth if for no other reason than sheer pig-headedness. The woman was no longer as important as the winning.

Several men standing next to Leonardo whispered to him that that man was known to be a big gambler and a bad man to have as an enemy. There were many stories around about dark nights and knives in the backs of people who went up against him.

Leonard ignored the conversations going on around him as he continued to bid on Mona, the slave girl. The bidding continued to rise, until finally Leonardo removed his money purse from its holding belt, and walked slowly and deliberately up to the auctioneer who was standing at the front edge of the slave block.

He opened his purse and poured directly into the outstretched palm of the sweating auctioneer a rainbow of gold and silver coins, enough to make him a wealthy man for the rest of his life. Deep inside, Leonardo hoped that this seller of women would somehow die before sundown. His hatred for the slave system was that strong, but ignoring his own feelings, he continued with his deeply felt desire to purchase the girl.

The Arab on the other side of the auction block gave up. He would have his vengeance against Leonardo another day. To go up any higher on his already-overpriced bid would have broken him completely, and to him, no mere female was worth it. He turned angrily, with his robes whipping about him, as he stalked off.

The now-smiling auctioneer handed Leonardo the title to his new female acquisition.

Leonardo asked what the she-savage's name was, and from where had she come. He learned that she had been picked up

13

on a slaving raid in the mountains of Armenia, and that was all that the auctioneer knew about her.

The auctioneer wished the Great Lord Leonardo good luck with her. He did say that her name was Monaphia, and did the Great Lord want his personal brand put on her so that she would be returned to him whenever she would run away?

Leonardo told him no. He did not want any more marks on her body.

Monaphia stood there in absolute silence as she listened to the exchange between the auctioneer and her new master. She was watching Leonardo with obvious contempt on her face.

Leonardo vividly recalled that when he came near her, the smell of her drove him back. The auctioneer apologized, saying that the wench refused to do anything about cleanliness, and had badly scratched one of his eunuchs when he attempted to bathe her. After that they just left her alone.

Leonardo took hold of the rope leash that was attached to the slave ring around her neck, and jerked her from the stage without giving her a chance to do or say anything. Keeping the rope taut, he made his way through the laughing crowd, making sure she was well behind him so that he would not have to smell her.

The four bodyguards, always at his side for security purposes, normally walked a few feet behind him. Now, however, they all wisely moved in front of Leonardo and led the way back to his castle.

The castle itself was made of stone and was protected by high turrets and a large water-filled moat to keep un-wanted guests away. Leonardo had armored men who stood guard twenty-four hours a day to defend the da Vinci stronghold against any possible enemies. Inside his castle lived a very self-sufficient feudal community which was able to withstand an attack from the outside for many months if need be. Even Leonardo da Vinci had enemies, and if nothing else in his life, Leonardo was cautious.

This part of central Florence was in hilly country, and Leonardo had built his castle on a high, rocky point from which all attackers would have difficulty approaching. The deep-water moat surrounding the entire castle had a single drawbridge that could be lifted or lowered only from within the castle. This effectively guarded the entrance and prevented unwanted visitors.

It was into this castle that the little group of warriors, the woman and Leonardo entered.

§

Now that he had them all back safely within his castle, Leonardo dismissed the guards.

Several minutes later found Mona standing in the center of his large living room, looking around like a wary and very frightened animal. Her eyes darted back and forth as if she were looking for a weapon or an easy way of escape.

Leonardo completely ignored her and ordered the household servants to draw warm water for the bathtub which stood off to the corner of the large room. While this was being done, Leonardo changed into a more practical costume for the forthcoming job. Clad only in a loincloth, he walked back into the main room where she was still standing.

Mona saw him coming and drew back half-frightened at the sight of the man in front of her, and yet, at the same time, completely fascinated. She had never seen a body-builder's body before, and the new master standing before her was a twisted and knotted interesting mass of muscles. She watched him carefully, becoming aware that even though he was so heavily muscled, he moved and flowed like a cat.

Leonardo recalled standing directly in front of her and locking his eyes on her. His grey-blue eyes were looking into her almond-brown ones. He spoke to her directly for the first time: "Woman, you will wash yourself."

She brought up some reserve courage and spat at him, and as she spat, a hard hand knocked her to her knees.

He repeated his command: "Woman, you will wash yourself! I will not tolerate your foul manners," he shouted.

Mona rushed at Leonardo, fingers like claws, going for his eyes. She suddenly found her wrists locked in a steel grip. Her body twisted around as Leonardo wrapped his other hand into her long hair. He threw her violently to the floor and dragged her by the greasy locks of her filthy head to where the steaming tub was waiting.

Since the household staff was afraid to touch her, Leonardo dismissed them all and then began to strip away the remaining tattered pieces of clothing from her body. He paused and had to catch his breath as he saw her fully for the first time.

She was like a panther, all female, with lean rippling flesh and beautiful firm breasts. She barely came up to his shoulders, but all of her was ready to fight. What an incredible woman!

He raised her clear of the ground by her hair until her feet were dangling uselessly beneath her. Now she was unable to resist any of his efforts as he swung her directly into the foaming hot water. A moment later he jumped in after her.

She immediately started to fight Leonardo as she struggled against him.

He quickly stopped her new efforts by forcing her head under water and held her there until he saw air bubbles rising from her. He then raised her out of the water to breathe and repeated this action over and over until she was finally too weak for any further resistance.

He washed her then, with his own hands, just as he would have washed a baby. He took absolutely no liberties with her. He was very careful and methodical as he scrubbed her hair again and again until he finally was able to rinse out all of the grease and accumulated dirt. Then he began to work on her skin. After scrubbing off the layers of dirt and grime, he rubbed her skin into a pink healthy glow.

In spite of herself, Mona began to relax. She was so very tired. It had been a long struggle since she had been captured, and she gave in to Leonardo's unrelenting hands that were now becoming gentler as she resisted him less. His hands kneaded and stroked gently with a sense of familiarity. She felt like a baby in his hands, and he was treating her with extra care and great thoughtfulness. Even when he washed her breasts, his heavily scarred hands displayed no interest to suggest he was enjoying her helplessness, and in a distant corner of her mind this bothered her.

When the bath was completed, Leonardo raised her from the soapy water and called for fresh jars of warm water to rinse them both off.

When Mona was done, a warm robe was brought to wrap around her nakedness, and he escorted her to a small side room where a sleeping pallet was laid out as a day bed. Mona began to tense up. This was to be it. He was going to take her now.

But Leonardo surprised her once again when he suddenly turned and walked out of the sleeping room, leaving her all alone on the pillowed pallet. From where she lay, she could see that he had returned to his own room, and had closed the curtain behind him.

Mona was confused. Why had he bought her if he did not desire her? Why would he pay such a great price for her and then just ignore her? She was beginning to feel pride in the fact that her master had paid a thousand times more for her than anyone had ever paid for a slave girl before. It was all so strange and confusing to her.

Her eyes closed. She was tired, so very tired. Still very confused, she was not aware of the moment when sleep finally overcame her. In spite of it all, the bath had taken some of the tension from her body, and she slept peacefully and deeply.

In the meantime, Leonardo had called for his favorite wine, and had the lamps lit in his room. He was sitting on several soft cushions, trying to answer the same question for himself that

Mona had previously pondered upon. He sat up all that night thinking and cursing at himself for being such a fool.

What was there about this woman? He realized that she could be more trouble than she was probably worth. For the amount of money he had spent on her, he could have purchased an entire harem made up of beautiful, good-natured wenches who would have been delighted to serve him.

There was, however, something very special about this woman. Was it pride? She had continued to fight even though she was definitely terrified. She had fought in the only way that she knew how and she was damned good at it.

He had no business getting emotionally involved with this woman! The only thing that she would bring him in the end was sorrow. Still, there was something special about her that cried out to him.

§

Leonardo had to fight off the urge to enter her room and lie beside her. He knew that he could take her anytime he wanted, but he also knew that there would be no pleasure in the taking, since she would give him absolutely nothing of her inner self. He might enter her body, but that would be all. He would not be able to touch her mind or her soul. He cursed himself again and wondered aloud why that should make a difference to him, but it did.

Once while she was sleeping, he saw her shivering from the cold night air. He brought her a warm covering and laid it gently upon her so as not to awaken her. Her face was so angelic in sleep. She was absolutely beautiful and probably no more than twenty years of age. By comparison, Leonardo felt old at twenty-three, old in the way that trees, stones, and mighty civilizations are old.

The night wore on and he dozed in his separate room while the oil lamps threw shadows against the walls. He was still sitting there when dawn began to brighten the skies.

Mona awoke with a start. Her eyes, at first, showed panic. She removed the covering from her and wondered from where it had come.

Rising, she unconsciously touched her hair as she moved the curtain aside and walked over to the room from where she had seen Leonardo enter. She watched him sleep for a few moments before the rustling of the curtain that she was holding woke him.

His eyes jerked wide open at the sound, and he immediately looked at her. He then nodded his head as if to verify a decision that he had already made.

Leonardo motioned for her to come to him. She obeyed, walking stiff-legged as a frightened fawn might, for there was power in the man she was staring at. He motioned for her to kneel, and she again obeyed, wondering why she was not resisting his orders. His rough hands reached ever so slowly around her neck, and with a twisting motion, his fingers tore apart the slave collar that she had been wearing.

Lying on the table next to him was the ownership deed the auctioneer had given him. Leonardo unrolled the document, took an inked writing stylus, and after making some marks on the scroll, signed his name and rank.

Mona watched, wondering just what it was that Leonardo was doing. Wearily he handed the document to her.

"Here, take it, Mona! I am giving you your freedom. I will not have that which is not freely given, and I feel it is best that you leave and return home to your family. Surely if you were to stay, you would bring me nothing but pain." In contrast to his rough handling of her the night before, Leonardo's words were spoken gently.

She knew now that Leonardo wanted her, and that he could have easily taken her, but she was very pleased that he had not done so. Mona put the document of her freedom inside her robe, saying nothing more. She was confused.

She looked deeply into his eyes, and saw something she had never seen before in a man. There was a terrible sadness about him, and his eyes looked as if he had known suffering far deeper than she had ever known.

She saw something else in those almost blue eyes when he looked at her. She saw the beginning of love. That must have been why Leonardo was setting her free. Being a woman, she knew that he was afraid of falling in love with her. At that moment, the heart within her went out to him.

He waved his hand, and said in a gentle voice, "Go from here now." He tossed her a heavy bag of silver coins. "This will get you back to your people. Go! Leave me now." He placed his head between his hands, his elbows on the table, and refused to look at her again.

Mona rose, silently holding the bag of silver in her hands, and walked out of the room.

He signed again and let his breath out slowly. His eyes were heavy from lack of sleep. He laid his head down on the table and fell asleep once more. Mona was gone.

§

A tinkling sound awoke Leonardo sometime later. His eyes were heavy with unfinished sleep as he tried to focus on his surroundings. He saw a small sparkle, and then another as silver coins fell into a pile in front of him.

Mona was kneeling beside him and when the last coin had fallen from the pouch to join the others on the table and floor, she dropped the bag on top of them and touched Leonardo with her hand.

She rested her small fingers on top of his and said in a soft voice, "You are still tired, my master. Please come and lie with me."

Mona had tried to leave when Leonardo had sent her

away, but something had drawn her back. Three times she had walked away only to find herself, again and again, standing in the doorway to Leonardo's room.

She had returned, ignoring the questioning looks of those within his household. She wanted to learn more about Leonardo. She took his hand, and this time she did the leading as she guided him to her bed.

Heavily, Leonardo lay down, and she put herself beside him, her heart beating wildly, her mind surprised at what she was actually doing.

She waited for him to take her. She had never had a man before, though many had tried. She had fought them all so savagely that they had left her alone and gone in search of easier pickings.

Now she waited. She almost panicked and wanted to run as his muscled arm went around her shoulders and drew her to him, but his arm was gentle and simply pulled her closer to him. She had decided that she was not running this time.

Her head was against Leonardo's chest, her face against his soft skin. The manly smell of him was in her nostrils as she waited for his hands to strip her of the robe that she wore. But those hands never came. He had fallen asleep while he was holding her gently in his arms.

She relaxed finally, moving her face so that her hair was out of the way and she placed her face and mouth next to his chest. Then she, too, slept! She slept in the arms of the man who had bought her, freed her, and then sent her away. Knowing that Leonardo had not forced her, and his possessive embrace of her, drew her to him more closely than any other act could have.

They slept long and deeply, each next to the other. It was nightfall before they awakened and looked at each other. Both of them were surprised at what they saw in each other's face.

When she snatched a shaky breath and inhaled the masculine scent of him, she experienced a strange heat deep inside of her. Butterflies rioted in her stomach as her eyelashes fluttered up to meet those fathomless pools within his eyes. Mona felt as if she were being absorbed into the depths of those spellbinding eyes, as if her energy was flowing into him like a swift current following the channel of a river. When his full lips descended upon hers in the slightest whisper of a kiss, Mona felt herself melting.

He was without a doubt, the most perfect male specimen on whom she had ever feasted her eyes. This warrior was a living column of imposing strength with greatly proportioned shoulders and a chest like solid rock. His muscular body glided over hers for a moment before he pulled back like an outgoing tide. Then he kissed her again, deeply kissed her.

Mona felt a wild, uncontrollable tremor flooding through her body followed by a wave of panic that accompanied those soul- shattering sensations.

Before she lost her composure, Leonardo backed away. He knew that he was daring too much, too quickly with one so inexperienced in the deep intimacies between a man and a woman.

Mona swallowed hard, trying to ignore the many tingling sensations that spilled through her body. She very nearly leapt out of her skin when Leonardo touched the peak of her breast and lifted his questioning brow. His blue- gray eyes twinkled but no smile crossed his lips. Mona thought she was going to die of embarrassment at the familiarity of his touches. Her modesty was the price she knew she had to pay to establish a bond between herself and her magnificent master.

Mona found herself gently drawn down onto the quilt. His hard-muscled flesh half-covered her and heightened her awareness of this intriguing man, who was a paradox of tenderness and omnipotent strength. She sighed audibly as she felt an indescribable longing inside her. His complete gentleness stripped away her inhibitions as if they had never existed.

When his mouth covered hers in a tender but possessive

kiss, Mona surrendered without a fight. He had taught her not to fear him, and she responded with an ever-growing sense of trust and a burning desire to investigate the mystical dimensions of these pleasurable sensations.

When Leonardo's hand glided up her thigh, Mona felt that her flesh was about to melt off her bones. His complete explorations of her body spurred a need that was fast becoming an addiction within her. His caress was so gentle and unhurried that she was helpless to object. Her mouth opened to the silent urging of his kiss.

Their tongues met, their breaths merged, his hands skimmed over her flat stomach and Mona felt warm tingles awakening her body. When his hands scaled the ladder of her ribs to swirl over her breasts, Mona felt hot desire riveting her naïve body. She arched helplessly toward him, granting him privileges he had not yet requested. His hands and lips were teaching her startling discoveries about intimacy, and she instinctively responded to them.

What was the matter with her, she wondered. The way she shamelessly yielded to his tender touch, one would have thought that this was far from her first time.

Leonardo lowered his head to brush his lips over the soft pink buds of her breasts, savoring the texture and scent of her skin. His tongue flicked out to tease the rigid peaks, and he felt her luscious body quiver in response. When he suckled the dusky crest, her body instinctively moved toward his.

Her arms glided over his shoulders, and she trembled from the need that was mounting within her. Her breath lodged in her throat when his hands and lips feathered over her body, finding and sensitizing every single inch of her flesh.

Mona could form no protest as Leonardo explored her completely. A flood of desire stained her cheeks while she watched his eyes travel from the top of her head to the tips of her toes.

Sensations spilled through her just as he reached out to

caress her once again. Part of her was thoroughly ashamed at her lack of feminine reserve, and another part of her simply defied conscience and restraint. She was aching to discover where these delicious sensations would lead.

§

Until this very moment, Mona had been naively unaware of the powerful undercurrent of desire that could draw a woman into such hazy depths and simply drown her. Over and over again, languid kisses and caresses flooded over her naked flesh.

Mona became the center of a pulsating awareness that throbbed in spellbinding rhythm. She gave herself up to the wild, mindboggling sensations that made her realize that she had come to life for the very first time. She was astonished by the maelstrom of emotions she never knew existed, and she actually arched for more of this wondrous torment.

A gasp tumbled from her lips when his caresses became far more urgent, far more erotic. He guided her thighs apart with his knees and bent to spread a row of heated kisses over her stomach and the downward curve of her hips. When his hand glided lower, Mona completely forgot how to breathe or why she needed to. These remarkable sensations were more than enough to sustain her.

Her body shuddered in uncontrollable spasms when his fingertips began to explore the very essence of her femininity. He stroked her, aroused her, until she began to convulse around him, lost in sweet torturous pleasure. Suddenly his intimate caresses were not enough to satisfy the monstrous ache that was swallowing her alive. Mona clutched at him, her nails digging into the very scars on his shoulders.

When Leonardo drew Mona's quivering hand across the velvet length of him, the breath she had been holding gushed out of her in a ragged sigh. She was touching him where he was most a man, and it sent her senses reeling, escalating her own pleasure.

She dared the inconceivable, and yet it still did not satisfy the white-hot need that coursed through her. When Leonardo showed her how to please him with her untutored caresses, she gave no thought to right or wrong, only to the compelling powers of passion in its purest and most unselfish form.

Mona soared at this newfound power she suddenly held over this magnificent giant. For all his brute strength, he had suddenly become her slave, moving upon her command. It was as if he had begun to live through her touch, and touch him she did, with caresses and kisses that expressed her own need to return the pleasure he had bestowed upon her.

She wanted him to know how he had affected her. She watched him succumb to her bold caresses as completely as she had succumbed to his.

Leonardo rolled above her while she held the pulsating length of him in her hand. He ached to feel more than just the throbbing need of his desire surrounded by her fingertips. He wanted to become part of her for one great and glorious moment that would capture time itself. His arms trembled as he held himself above her, refusing to frighten her and yet aching to devour her completely.

Mona flinched when she felt the penetrating length of him searing into her like velvet fire. Sharp pain shattered the magical spell that she was under, and she instinctively began to push him away.

"No—stop! You are hurting me!"

Leonardo had depleted every ounce of self-restrain that he possessed. He could feel his passion spurring him on like a merciless rider. This, Leonardo decided, was the absolute worst kind of torture a man could endure.

He could not hold himself in check a moment longer. His need had become so tangible that it crippled his mind and body. He would make this lovely siren forget the initial pain when he swept her up with him to heights of pleasure that would be absolutely unbelievable.

As for Mona, she swore that her body had split wide open as Leonardo thrust deeply into her tender flesh. She could not draw a breath nor move on her own. The pain intensified as he glided into her with steady rocking motions that pressed her deeper and deeper into the bed.

A hoarse cry tumbled from her lips but Leonardo smothered it with his possessive kisses. He shared his breath when she could grasp none or her own, and then … the most paradoxical sensation claimed her. An exquisite pleasure born of pain flooded over her.

Mona could feel herself accepting his entry like a new blossom unfolding in the warmth of the morning sun. It was as if her naive body had suddenly acquired an instinct that had before been unknown to her. She began to move in rhythm with Leonardo, meeting each of his hard-penetrating thrusts.

She was compelled by some nameless sensation that expanded at a phenomenal rate—like a ball of fire consuming all within its path and feeding on its own raging flames.

Mona felt like a meteor blazing across the sky and charting a course to its very own destruction. Sensation after sensation converged upon her, until she cried out in the overwhelming wonder of it all.

She swore that she had left her scratch marks on this noble warrior, when another spasm of rapture riveted her. Her nails spiked into the tendons of his powerful arms. Her legs curled around him, holding him, arching ever closer to the maddening need that engulfed her. Every ounce of self-control abandoned her.

The hypnotic sensations had recoiled upon her as they bombarded her at the same breathless moment. Wild spasms raced through every nerve and muscle, and Mona clung to Leonardo as if he were the only force in the swirling universe that had any meaning. Indeed, at that moment he was her only sanity. She was living and dying in the same fantastic moment!

When his powerful body shuddered upon her, another wave

of sensations crested over her, stripping every last fragment of thought from her mind. For what seemed like forever, Mona laid there, her body intimately joined with his, as if she were a living, breathing part of the incredible Leonardo da Vinci.

A lazy smile pursed her lips as her hand absently trailed across his hip to investigate the corded muscles of his back. How very easy, she thought, to fall in love with a man such as this—this gentle giant of a lover!!!

On those contented thoughts, Mona drifted off to sleep to relive in her dreams, the erotic events that she had just experienced. She could vividly see those twinkling blue-gray eyes of his reaching out to her across a sea of delicious memories.

THE WILD, WILD WEST

1875 TO 1879

INTRODUCTION TO THE WILD, WILD WEST

Following the Civil War, thousands of adventurous men, veterans from both the Union and the Confederate armies, moved west. The time frame was from 1875 to 1879. The West offered fresh opportunities. There was land out there for the taking, and a chance for these men to start their lives all over again.

Above all, with the War between the States finally over, the country was filled with a restlessness, and people felt the need to accomplish something on their own. This desire to do something "better" was evident in more ways than just searching for land, cattle or gold.

These former soldiers were no longer content to be what they had been before the war. They had fought shoulder to shoulder with men who were better educated and had greater experience with life. They wanted a piece of the great American dream for themselves.

The future out west seemed more promising to these returning soldiers than just going back to the small farms where they had grown up. These were men who did not fear the unknown, and were not overcome by great distances or the vastness of the skyline. They knew in their hearts that the West was where they belonged, and that this wide-open land and all that it contained was theirs for the taking.

Of all the wild characters of the western frontier, the gunfighter was the most feared and flamboyant.

They were not simply violent, because in a violent age this was hardly unique. As the editor of the *Kansas City Journal* remarked in 1881, "The gentleman who has killed his man is by no means a rare specimen." This very same man is met daily on Main Street in the various walks of life.

The gunfighters whose reputations have survived all had some very defining characteristic: depravity, good looks, courage, mystery, vicious temper, sadism, marksmanship, or dandyism. In fact, the term "gunfighter" did not come into popular use until the 1870s.

It was Bat Masterson, who wrote articles for a local newspaper, who gave his first-hand accounts of the luminaries of the West. But he generally preferred to use the term "mankillers." The earlier terms used to describe a man who lived by his gun, were either "man-killer" or "shootist." These "shootists" were an integral part of the West, and a direct result of the conditions there.

The rule of law governed disputes in the eastern united states, while the gun was the "western arbiter" of choice. Gunfighters worked on both side of the legal divide! They worked as both lawmen or criminal outlaws. Many changed sides when it suited them. Most were motivated by money and were only loyal to their own interests.

Gunfighters themselves came from a wide sweep of backgrounds. They ranged from men available as "guns for hire" in range wars, to specific contract killers. The term "gunfighter" was also used to cover men who fought in gunfights, but these were far less frequent than might be supposed from Western films and dime novels.

In countless Western movies, the "gunslinger" twirls his pistols around, does trick shooting, and generally shows off his prowess with his weapons. In real life, gunmen almost never squared off against each other in the shootouts that are so popular in western films and literature. Gunfighters had far too much respect for each other's skills to risk it, knowing that a real gunfight would be fatal for at least one of the duelists, if not both. Indeed, well-known gunfighters were held in such general fear that they were very rarely challenged by anyone who knew their reputations.

This then, will be two adventures taken out of the life story of "Big Ed" Johnson. Author Bud Seligson is in the process of compiling Big Ed's life story and allowed two of his many adventures to be used in this storyline to show that Big Ed lived his life to the fullest extent possible.

BIG ED JOHNSON & MAY LING

BIG ED JOHNSON AND HIS INTRODUCTION TO
DEADWOOD, SOUTH DAKOTA — AND THE FAMOUS
FEMALE CHINESE BEAUTY KNOWN AS MAY LING. A
SHORT AND VERY PASSIONATE LOVE STORY BY BUD
SELIGSON

§

The year is 1877. Cowboys and cattle drives are dominating the wild, wild West!

The town of Deadwood, South Dakota, lay sprawled in its own lazy and quiet comfort along the banks of a large creek called West Water. The town's large main street crossed the creek at a right angle from one end of the small town to the other.

The ancient stone stage-coach station, a veteran of the famous local Indian wars, stood quietly near the east bank of the flowing river. It was a low-roofed, single-storied building, with an awning that projected eight feet from the roof, offering shelter to a couple of initial-carved wooden benches huddled beneath its shiny polished surface. Opposite the stage station was the local sheriff's office and jail, which faced the local assayer's office. Just beyond them were a real-estate office and the large Diamond Palace saloon and gambling hall.

It was what was beyond all of these front-sided structures

that had caught Big Ed's eye. There was a small, low-standing building with a big sign on it that read *Public Baths—Open to One and All!* He was just riding slow and easy when he first saw the sign, which brought a big smile to his rugged face. Both Big Ed and his horse were extremely dust-covered, and they were both uncomfortable about it.

He rode directly to the stables, and after dismounting, walked his tired stallion over to the handler, who took a small gold piece and heard his request to give the horse a wash, a rubdown, and a quiet stall for the night. He also ordered the best hay and oats that could be provided for him. Big Ed was a firm believer in keeping his horse and his weapons in first-class order.

It was then that Ed turned his attention to the bathhouse, as the stable hand watched him walk away with the tell-tale walk of a professional gunman. His profession seemed to be marked by the two tied-down six-shooters that he wore low down on his hips.

§

Big Ed was starting to feel like a new man! The trail dust, dirt and grime were soaking off his body into the soapy water at the Deadwood Bathhouse. He had showered first, then spent the next hour in an oversized iron bathtub filled with hot soapy water.

The bath was a wonderful beginning for what he hoped would be a lucky visit to the world-famous gambling casino located just down the street. The Casino/Saloon had earlier that year acquired a world-famous reputation by being the location where James Butler Hickok, also known as Wild Bill Hickok, was shot in the back while playing poker.

Wild Bill was the last to sit in on a game of five-card draw poker, and he had to take the only players' seat that was open at that moment. That was the seat with his back to the swinging doors that led in from the outside street. From where Wild Bill was sitting, he could not see anyone coming up behind him.

Several days before that fatal poker game, he had acted in his capacity as the town's United States Marshal when he had jailed a nobody and charged him with being drunk and disorderly in a public place. This person, upon being released from the holding cell, had put on his guns and walked straight over to the saloon where the card game was going on. He walked up to Wild Bill, who could not see him coming, and shot him point-blank in the back of the head.

Wild Bill was, of course, pronounced dead at the scene, and what quickly became famous was the poker hand that he was holding when he was shot. Of the five cards in his hand, he had two aces and two eights. The fifth card remains unknown. From that day forward, aces and eights have been known as The Dead Man's Hand.

It was Big Ed's desire to sit in on a poker game at the same table where Wild Bill was killed. He just wanted to see the famous location before he continued on with his journey west.

The smiling Oriental gentleman who softly padded into the soaking room broke into Ed's thoughts. He was the owner of the establishment, and he was there to add another bucket of hot water to the soaking tub. He went in and out of the side room where a large stove would heat up the water for the baths.

The little man was dressed in all-black "coolie" clothes. He had established the bathhouse when the city of Deadwood became the end of the cattle trail from Texas and the surrounding areas. Horsemen who came to Deadwood from all different directions always arrived with a thick layer of trail dust, just like Big Ed. These men always made the bathhouse their first stop in the cow town.

"Is your business doing good"? Big Ed asked.

"Business good," smiled the old man. "No time eat lunch! Me go eat now! Go home and take nap!"

"You want me to get out?" asked Big Ed.

"No, no!" The man clasped his hands together and bowed

down low. "Honorable customer enjoy bath! May Ling wash and iron your clothes! She in back! You need anything, yell loud for May Ling!" The smiling Chinaman again bowed low and backed himself out of the room. He disappeared behind a pair of bright red beaded curtains.

Big Ed laid his head on the folded towel on the back of the tub. He closed his eyes and relaxed. His moment of silence was ended by a delicate cough coming from the rear of the room. He glanced up as the curtain parted and a petite Chinese girl came into the room.

She was wearing a floor-length green and red silk robe with Oriental symbols of dragons embroidered on it. The young woman averted her eyes as she approached Big Ed's tub.

"Papa go to lunch," she said. "May Ling is boss now! May Ling put closed sign on door. We alone in here. You want more hot water?"

"Naw, I'm about done," Big Ed said. "Another ten minutes and I'll turn into a prune!"

She smiled. "May Ling think you dirty man!"

Big Ed looked her over carefully. "So you are the famous May Ling?" He was very pleased with the way she looked. He especially liked her sparkling black eyes and her golden skin. "Maybe you could wash my back"?

"At honorable customer's service!" The girl bowed low with a mocking smile on her pretty face. "What customer want, he get. Honorable father teach May Ling how to please."

Big Ed grinned. "Is that a fact?"

"Is true!"

"Your father is a very wise man."

"May Ling think so!" She picked up a long-handled brush from a shelf above the big tub and began to brush Big Ed's back with a very vigorous motion.

Big Ed sighed. "You have a very nice touch, May Ling."

"You have nice body, Mr. Cowboy! May Ling like hard bodies!"

"Shucks, May Ling! I'll bet you say that to all of your customers.

"Not true," the Chinese girl protested. "May Ling peek when you take off clothes. You have very nice body! You big man."

Big Ed laughed. "Thank you very much."

"Is true!" May Ling giggled.

She laid down the brush and picked up a cake of soap. "May Ling soap you up good."

Big Ed stretched out in the iron bathtub as May Ling's hand dipped beneath the foamy surface of the bathwater. Her palm glided down across Big Ed's hard stomach.

"Real big one!" said May Ling. "You want to do it?"

"You are reading my mind!"

May Ling's hand came up out of the water. She pulled a towel off a nearby rack. "Get dry. We go in back room. May Ling show you Oriental mystery."

Big Ed stood up in the bathtub with water pouring off of his body. He reached for the towel, but May Ling shook her head negatively. She came forward and rubbed a warm towel over his skin, first gently and then with a stronger pressure.

"Umm, that feels good!" Big Ed said.

"You follow May Ling now." The young Chinese woman took Big Ed's hand and led him through the beaded curtain into the back room.

This area of the building contained a large iron stove, several different sizes of washtubs, and an ironing board. He saw his clothes hanging neatly. They were washed, ironed and ready to wear.

"We go to parlor," May Ling said. She took Big Ed's hand and led him through another pair of thick curtains. "This May Ling's favorite room! I do best work here."

Big Ed felt as if he were entering an Oriental temple dedicated to love-making. There were lots of colorful Chinese pictures showing men and women in various stages of love-making. In the center of the room was a single, thickly padded mattress that was covered with a dark silk fabric. The mattress was surrounded by several black straw screens, woven to represent priceless tapestries. A black-lacquered chest and a small chair were the only other furniture in the room.

"You like?" May Ling asked.

"Beautiful!"

"May Ling want you be happy. Please lie down."

Following her directions, Big Ed eased his long, naked body down on the mattress.

May Ling giggled. "You too tall, cowboy," she whispered, pointing at Big Ed's feet that were sticking out over the end of the mattress. "You like feel of silk on skin?"

Big Ed wiggled on the silk coverlet. "Very smooth."

"How 'bout this feel?"

May Ling knelt beside him, and her fingers grasped his swelling erection. She watched as the flesh hardened and lengthened under her practiced touch.

"You're a wonderment," Big Ed said.

"Ummm," was the only comment May Ling made as her head dipped low, her lips open wide to take in the full length of him.

The sensation was wonderful as her warm mouth slowly engulfed his pulsating flesh. Her tongue made a series of tiny movements, calculated and deliberate, like an Oriental butterfly's wings fluttering in the wind.

Next, the intensity of her mouth increased, and Big Ed's body arched up to meet her. Then, with a pleasurable release, he was freed from his tension.

He looked down and the only thing he could see was May Ling's mass of black hair.

The Chinese girl turned around and grinned up at him. "Welcome to Deadwood," she said. "What your name?"

"Just call me Lucky!"

CALAMITY JANE

AND NOW THAT WE'VE HAD SOME FUN WITH BIG ED AND MAY LING, LET US GET INTO THE STORY ABOUT THE GREAT LADY KNOWN TO HISTORY AS CALAMITY JANE

By the time he was a teenager, Big Ed knew everything that there was to know about a deck of playing cards.

He knew that in a game of draw poker, when holding a pair and drawing three cards, his chances of making three of a kind were exactly three hundred and fifty-nine to one against him. He also knew all about cheating, and he could detect the very whisper of a card being dealt from the bottom of the deck with the best of them.

His paternal grandfather, the head of the Johnson clan, was a small-time gambler, and he took on the job of making Ed into a good gambler. "Take this deck of cards," he would tell Ed. "Shuffle them a hundred times each night before you go to sleep. Learn the feel of them and learn to handle them quickly and easily. Even if you never play cards, it will make your fingers more agile and your eyes quicker. It can never hurt you to gain a new skill."

And so it was to be. Night after night, he would practice until he could handle the cards smoothly and with great dexterity. He was taught how to deal, second-deal, and to deal off the bottom of the deck.

His grandfather taught him how to cut cards and re-shift the cut back to where he wanted it to be. "A gentleman never cheats, Ed," his grandfather would always say to him. "But sometimes you will not be playing cards with completely honest players, and in order for you not to be cheated, you must know what it is that the cheater can do. If you suspect a game of being "cooked," get out of that game and get out fast! Use any excuse you can come up with, but get out of that game!

"Train your memory, and learn how to watch everything that is going on around you at that poker table. Be able to recall every card that has been played in each hand that you are in on.

"And most importantly, notice the people, places and things. This could save your life."

§

And so, there I was, Big Ed Johnson, sitting in the exact same seat that Wild Bill Hickok sat in on the day he was killed. I was sitting at the same table with my back also to the swinging doors, and I just sat there for a moment or two, just watching this here "slick" gambling man palming an ace from the bottom of the deck.

It was not as if I hadn't told him straight out, quite clearly and directly to the point. I stepped back from that there poker table, and said, clear as all daylight, to him and to all the others who were gathered around us just a-watchin' and a-listenin', "Mister gambling man," I said, "if you ain't any slicker using that there six shooter of yours, then you were with that sloppy ace that you just pulled from the bottom of that deck of cards, then you'd better not have at it with me."

The trouble was that he wasn't happy making just one mistake, but he had to go on and make it two in a row! So when he pulled that pistol of his and faced me across that green-covered poker table, I found him out to be as bad with a pistol as he was at double-dealin' from the bottom of that poker deck.

That there bullet that I shot him with got him ready for a burial at Boot Hill, on the south side of town. That was where they buried men of poor judgement and a mighty slow draw.

And me, Big Ed Johnson, who came to town as a stranger and all alone, suddenly found myself a famous "talked-about man. I suddenly had this here instant reputation because of that fair fight, and my quick draw over that misunderstanding at that card game.

Now I don't mind being known as a fast draw and things like that, but loose talk sometimes gets things twisted around. So, right then and there, I decided that first thing tomorrow morning, it would be right proper and smart for me to become a wandering man again.

Kindly understand that I was no hero, and did not want to be one. All I wanted at that moment was to look right through my horse's ears at a lot of new real estate.

I suddenly realized how much I missed bedding down at night to the sounds of leaves rustlin', or runnin' water moving along with me where-ever I was going. I loved to get up in the mornings to the wonderful smell of wood-smoke and bacon fryin' in the pan. I really liked the simple life.

So I decided to have a drink in the bar, and then follow that up with a good dinner and get to sleep early, so I could get a good jump on the day ahead.

It is interesting how plans change without notice.

§

I did walk into the bar end of the saloon, but before I was able to order anything, I saw *her*.

She was standin' all by herself at the other end of the long bar, facing me. She stood erect, with her chin lifted a little and one hand resting on the shiny part of the highly-polished surface of the bar-top.

I noticed that her skin was the color of old ivory, and her

hair, which was jet-black, was gathered in a loose knot at the nape of her slender neck. But it was her sparkling eyes that were the most attention-getting. They were hazel with tiny flecks of a darker color, and they were large and her lashes were long.

Her lips were full but quite beautiful, and there was a certain wistfulness in her face, a strange elusive charm that prevented the lips from being sensual. Her figure would have caused a gasp from a marble statue, for it was seductively curved, and when she moved, it was with a sinuous grace that was a delight to see.

She came forward toward me, and I found myself just staring into her amazing eyes.

"Buy a girl a drink, stranger?" were the first words I heard from her.

I smiled and nodded at a nearby table and turned my attention to the barkeeper as she walked across the room and sat down, waiting for me to return with the drinks.

When I asked the bartender about her, he told me that her name was Martha Jane Cannary. He said that she liked to be called by her nickname, which was Calamity Jane.

I asked the bartender to explain such an unusual name to me, and he told me a brief story about her.

He said that a few years ago, when Calamity was new to the town, she was invited to a party being given by the owner of the local *Deadwood Press* newspaper. He wrote an article in his newspaper the next day, saying that the party that he gave was extremely boring until Martha Jane arrived. As soon as she settled in, she moved everyone into a party mood, and they all had a wild and wonderful time for the rest of the evening. She was the absolute life of the party with her bad language, some local jokes and stories, and her extremely talented singing voice.

The article went on to say that she knew how to get everyone moving, and she was a blessed "calamity" on two feet. That nickname stuck, and from that time forward, she was known as Calamity Jane to the world, but just plain Martha to her personal friends.

I asked the bartender for two glasses and a bottle of the best whiskey in the house.

While he was putting everything together for me, I took the moment to look at the bottles of whiskey that he was reaching for. I knew that most of the first-choice whiskeys were a combination of pure alcohol with a little hot pepper added to give it a kick. Some bartenders would cut their cheap drinks with turpentine, ammonia, gunpowder or other additions. Some even tossed in a small amount of rat poison to add to the flavoring.

Whiskey brands had some mighty interestin' names on them as I read them while I waited patiently for my order from the bartender. I reckoned that the labeling was their way of giving their customers some truth in advertising. I saw names like Dead Dog, Six Feet Under, and the most famous one of all, Coffin Juice. There was a large hand printed sign hanging on the bar's mirror, that said that if you wanted the house special, you just had to ask for "Rot-Gut."

I had plenty of money in my pocket from the poker game, and I left a large gold coin on the bar. I took the two glasses and a bottle of the establishment's finest whiskey over to the pretty little lady who was a-sittin' there quietly waiting on me.

§

Calamity Jane really loved her whiskey! While we were sitting there talking, she was putting away shots of whiskey at a rapid rate.

I mostly sat there listening to her lively chatter and watching her down her whiskey.

A few important understandings came from our discussion as we sat there. First there was the monetary agreement that we arrived at for her services to be rendered in my bed.

She agreed to be my bed partner for the night, and she

would let me have my way with her as soon as we had our supper. She said the price was $50 in gold coin, and that would buy dinner, a nice room on the second floor, and one whole night with her if I could last until the sun came up.

I just smiled at her cute comments. I agreed to her terms but I gave her triple her asking price in the gold that I had won at Wild Bill's poker table.

She made the $150 in gold disappear very quickly, and her face was smiling at me from ear to pretty ear. I could just see her mind a-workin' on what she would be doing with this large amount of money.

She said that for this kind of payment, I could do anything I wanted with her and to her. She put no restrictions on me. She was one very happy lady!

While we were waiting for the dinner that we ordered to be served to us from the kitchen, she had me laughing and singing little songs with her. She loved to sing and tell her stories, and I just sat there looking at her and listening to her chatter away.

The favorite story I remember that she told me at dinner that night was the following one about the oldest profession in the world, which she called "rough-and-ready prostitution." Her story went something like this:

The War between the States, or the Civil War, as it is sometimes called, ended several years ago in 1865 with the surrender of General Robert E. Lee to General Grant.

A year or so before the deciding big battles were to be fought that ended the four-year war, one of General Grant's commanders complained that many of his soldiers were coming and going in and out of their encampment each night. This was a terrible thing to be happening, because the big battles would be coming up soon, and he needed his army at absolute full strength.

His investigation provided him with the answer to his up-and-down manpower problems. It seems that his men were sneaking in and out of the camp in the middle of the night and visiting the local prostitutes in the nearby city.

Now Commander Hooker could secure the camp so that no one could get in or out, or he could allow the women, or camp followers, as he called them, to come into the camp and spend their nights there. He decided to let the ladies come and go as they pleased, and in that way he always would know where his men would be when he needed them.

The system worked out so well that a new term described the local girls who provided these services to the soldiers and came and went as they wished: they became know as General Hooker's girls. In later years, when the term became more well-known to the public at large, these girls simply became known as "hookers."

Calamity Jane, with a great big smile on her pretty face, was pleased to tell me that "hooker" was the new popular word for the girls who worked in her chosen profession.

I laughed with her as we both dug into the dinner that had finally arrived.

§

Calamity had booked us into the best room in the saloon, which was on the walk-up second floor. She took out two keys and gave me one of them. She said that she needed to wash up, and she asked that I give her thirty minutes before I came up.

She described several outfits that she used for business, and asked which one I would like her to wear for our fun evening that was ahead of us. She seemed pleased with what

I suggested she wear. She kissed me softly on my cheek and headed up the stairs.

I just sat quietly for the half hour enjoying one of the local cigars, which the bartender brought over to me. The single gold coin that I had given him was going a long way.

I was getting excited just thinking that the rest of the night should prove out to be a lot of fun. Calamity was surely a fun kind of girl!

The thirty minutes had passed quickly, and I now found myself double-locking the door to the room that I had rented for the night.

§

I looked around for Calamity and noticed that she had pulled the bed covers down and placed a lot of small pillows at the top of the bed, which dominated the room.

The only light in the large room came from a dozen or more candles that all together gave the room a soft and quite romantic glow. Calamity had taken the time and energy to prepare our get-together perfectly.

I heard noises coming from out of the bathroom, and I called out to her in a loud enough voice to be heard inside the closed bathroom door. Suddenly, she slipped into the room, and she was beautiful, and I told her so.

"Martha Jane Cannary, you look lovely and absolutely radiant! I have never seen anyone look as desirable as you do right at this moment."

With the biggest smile on her face, she slowly stepped over to me in her bare feet. She was wearing a pair- of black stockings with matching garter belt, black panties, and a black frilly bra that pushed up her healthy breasts into a tantalizing showing of those desirable female weapons. She had completed her evening attire with a semi-open gray pullover sweater.

§

Not a word was spoken as Big Ed put his arms around her and carefully pulled her toward him. His breath was hot against her ear as he held her closely pressed against his body.

She smelled so good! He had the impression of roses and sweet perfume. He knew that he would smell of cigars, but that was just the way it was when a woman was for hire. After all, this was not a regular date back home on a Saturday night.

His hands slid slowly upward, carefully pulling the gray sweater up and over her head. Half the fun of making love to a woman was undressing her, and Ed wanted the sexual sensation. His hands threw the sweater across the room, away from them, as he softly kissed her ivory-white neck.

He ran his fingers up and down her back, and was pleased to feel her reaction to his touch. She was starting to respond to his gentle and slow approach, as his fingers sent shivers up and down her spine.

With no effort at all, he swept her off her feet, and carried her over to the big bed, where he placed her on her back so she would be looking up at him.

Gently he slid between her legs so that he was looking down at her. He was very careful not to put any of his weight on her as he simply gazed down into her eyes, which were watching his face.

Slowly he kissed her lips in the most tender of kisses, and quickly left them to continue on down to her throat, her soft shoulders, and finally he stopped his wandering with his head held just above her little peek-a-boo lacy bra.

It was time for the bra to go because it came between those sweet little peeking-out breasts and him. He could hardly wait to touch them. With no effort whatsoever, he flipped her over onto her stomach and undid the hook that held the bra encircling the most exciting part of the female figure. He completely ignored the now-useless bra and threw it across the room and out of his way.

Again effortlessly, he flipped her over to her back once more and put his arms around her as he pulled her toward him in what he intended to be a soft kiss.

Calamity obviously had other ideas. She took his free hand and placed it on one of her unobstructed breasts, and as she did so, she noted to herself that her nipples were getting hard and beginning to ache. She needed some relief from all this sexual foreplay. She was starting to get turned on by this slow-moving but gentle big guy.

She forced the issue of kissing into a long and drawn-out passionate session by using her tongue into and out of his mouth. One of her steady clients was a Frenchman who said that this hot type of kissing with tongues meeting was called French kissing." *Leave it to the French to come up with something like this,* she thought.

She pulled her head back for a moment and looked at his face. She was mighty pleased to see that his eyes had narrowed to mere slits, and his smile held a purely masculine look of triumph. It was exciting to see that she was pleasing the very best customer she'd had ever had!

She slipped away from his hands that were still freely roaming back and forth between her breasts. She jumped off the bed where she stood there with her hands on her hips, bare-breasted and wearing only stockings, garter belt, panties and a great big smile! Knowing that she had his full and undivided attention, she began to hum a dirty little song as she removed the rest of her clothes.

A few bumps and grinds later, and she was standing there naked before him. She was really enjoying herself with the slow but steady pace of their sexual encounter. Usually her customers were the "wham, bam, thank you, ma'am" kind of guys. She was actually having fun, and she felt herself getting hotter by the minute.

He looked really tall to her, and quite strong, and she knew that he stood well over six feet tall and towered over her. But then everyone looked tall to her as she was a small five foot one in height. Big as he was, she knew that she could handle his "passion puppy" with no problem when they finally did get around to it.

To move things along, she said in a soft and sexy voice, "Ed, now that you've seen me in all of my naked glory, how about my taking a look at your equipment? I always like to see what my bucking bronco looks like before I turn him loose!"

With a big grin on his face, it only took a few moments for Big Ed to be standing before her, as she would later say, "naked as a jay bird," and he was really something to see.

Calamity froze for a moment as she really took a good look at him.

This guy was freaking gorgeous, and he obviously knew what he wanted from her, and that was all right because it had been forever since she'd been properly "laid!"

What the hell, she thought as she watched him move. This might just be the highlight of her career as a hooker.

Ed's body looked like the professional boxer's body she had once seen when he was giving a boxing exhibition in the town square. He had the same deep, exquisitely defined chest muscles, with dark erect nipples. His arms and belly were corded with muscles that were unbelievable.

Calamity felt a wild flush race through her body. She was more than ready to jump into the sack even if he wasn't. She would have to move things along as he was definitely not the aggressive type.

Ed was saying, "You are quite lovely, Calamity! I'm going to enjoy having my way with you very much. But first, please come over here and kneel down."

Calamity was thinking, *Oh, my God, he doesn't want to screw me yet! He wants a blow job first.* She smiled to herself as she recalled saying that for the kind of money that he was paying her, he could have anything that he wanted from her. She knew that her enjoyment would come later. This was his time and she knew that this was something that she was very good at.

Calamity inhaled a deep breath and dropped to her knees in front of him. He probably had done this many times with lots of other girls, so she was going to see if she could give him something to remember her by.

He pushed his shaft down toward her lips. "Are you ready for me?" he asked in a husky voice.

Calamity stared at the cock pointed directly at her, and began to work her mouth to generate saliva. He was big: thick and long. That meant she could not take in his entire length as she had originally thought. She put her hands on him to control the length of him in order to make sure that he did not shove in any deeper than she could handle.

It was only a mere minute or two until he groaned, and his mouth gasped for breadth as he climaxed quickly.

That was too easy and too quick, she thought. She hoped that he could hold on longer when he finally made proper love to her.

Twenty minutes later found the two of them sitting together in the large bathtub provided for them in their rented room. Big Ed had the satisfied and contented look of a man who had just had his sexual fantasy satisfied, and he knew that Calamity was still eager to get him into her bed. She hadn't had anything done to her yet that would satisfy the sexual flush that he knew she was feeling.

§

Shortly, Big Ed was dressed and feeling like a million dollars!!!

He had just had a blow job from the most exciting girl in the world, and he was going down to the bar to get Calamity another bottle of whiskey and something for them both to eat. Then he planned to do some plain old-fashioned screwing.

Calamity was already in bed, and had the candlelight down low. The pillows were all propped up and ready for him to join her. She looked so sexy and exciting lying there that he hurried himself along and hustled out the door on his way down to the bar. It was not every night that he had an adorable young lady waiting to make love to him! Life was good.

GUNFIGHT AT THE O.K. CORRAL

SEVERAL WEEKS HAVE PASSED AND WE NOW
CONTINUE AND CONCLUDE THE STORY OF BIG ED.
THIS TIME WE MEET SUNNY THE BARTENDER AND
LEARN ALL ABOUT THE FAMOUS GUNFIGHT AT THE OK
CORRAL. A SHORT AND VERY PASSIONATE LOVE STORY
BY BUD SELIGSON

§

Big Ed Johnson, former captain of the Union Army, was walking his horse slowly down the last trail that led to the border-crossing into the Arizona Territory. He was in no hurry as he enjoyed the peace and quiet of the wilderness that was all around him.

He was more than pleased to watch the wild animals whose path they often crossed, as they dashed along living out their lives. He had recently encountered human beings who were wilder than those that he called animals, and he still wondered about the future of the human race. At least when an animal was violent, it was because they were either hungry or competing for a mate. Humans seemed to be violent for the very sake of violence itself. He was getting a headache thinking about all these things and decided to just continue living his life from one day to the next, letting things fall as they would.

Within the hour, he walked into the first saloon that the

great Territory of Arizona offered to the traveler, and he was mighty impressed. From the moment, he stepped through the swinging doors and on into the saloon itself, he had the feeling of simple elegance.

The first thing that caught his eye was the gigantic mirror that was divided into four equal parts and stretched the entire length of the long bar. The high ceiling was filled with hanging lamps that gave a glow to the highly-polished walls that reflected the brightness back into the large room. The floor was fitted, polished wood, and from the tops of the high oval windows, long drapes just barely kissed the wooden floor. It was an elegant look, and it made him think of some of the stories he had heard about Paris, France.

The next to the last feature of the room that most impressed him were the tables, which were scattered about the entire open space. They were made of hand-crafted heavy oak, padded in the seat and back areas. They were in soft colors that added to the over-all feelings of relaxation that the travelers were supposed to feel when they arrived at the end of their journey.

The final touch to all of the things that impressed him so much were the girls who were working behind the bar.

Big Ed was pretty much an expert on girls who worked the saloons for a living. He had been with the rough-and-ready Calamity Jane kind, Indian squaws, the soft and fluffy type of female, and the sweet, down-home-in-Tennessee kind of girls, who just wanted to have a drink and take you to their bed for a fee. He loved to love them all, and was always pleased to be with them.

But this collection of Arizona girls was different. He was beginning to think that maybe this was the place he was always looking for and could not find. It was going to be interesting to figure out!

But in the meantime, he needed to take a good look at the girls. It had been a while since he had been with a woman, and Ed always missed having one around.

First of all, he had to get used to the fact that all six of the bartenders were female. Not one man was in sight except for the two gents who were standing on the second-floor landings looking down at everything. Their job was to make sure that everyone conducted themselves in a proper manner. They look pretty nasty, and Big Ed thought that their looks alone should keep the peace.

Ed walked up to the perky blonde serving drinks from her section of the long bar. She looked to be in her early twenties, about five foot five or six, slim of body, with a great set of breasts that were well displayed! Big Ed always liked his women to be tall, slim, young and big-busted.

The funny thing, when he looked carefully at the blonde behind the bar, was that the other girls who were also serving drinks could have been her twins. They were dressed exactly the same, and physically, they had the same bodies. The only difference was that his choice was a blonde, and he also saw a redhead, a brunette, a strawberry blonde, and a pitch-black-haired one. The effect was amazing, and he saw that he now wasn't the only feller in the room looking at the bartenders.

Behind each girl on the glass mirror was a hand-printed cardboard sign that gave the girl's name and said in big letters that she was available if the price offered for her services was generous enough.

Ed had never seen anything like this before in all the years that he had been going into and out of saloons. It allowed the buyer to look over what the girls were selling before any offer was made. It seemed to be working out pretty well, as new girls kept coming out of the back room to replace the bartending girls who made a deal with one of their customers.

It was obvious that each girl had come to an understanding with one of the cowboys as they stepped away from the bar and led the gentleman up the rear stairs to where they probably fulfilled their agreements.

The blonde's name—or the name she had posted—was

Sunny! It seemed to fit her blond hair and great smile. Like all the other girls, she was dressed in a low-cut party dress that showed off her legs and breasts to great advantage.

Ed was mighty interested, and he made a good offer for her services, which she turned down.

Being turned down was a big surprise to him. Big Ed thought that one large gold coin would lock up the deal; after all, it had Calamity Jane all excited when he paid her price.

They discussed Sunny's fee back and forth for a little while, and since she looked so good, and he had visions of all kinds of sexy stuff dancing in his head, he finally accepted paying her two large gold coins and two small silver ones. Ed was thinking that she had better be the world's greatest lay for such a big expense. Ed, of course, did not say that out loud, but he was a-thinkin' that.

Sunny, Big Ed's new and most favorite bartender in the whole world, had a great smile on her face and a wiggle to her body that moved her breasts in such a way he almost jumped over the bar to grab ahold of them.

She told him that for the moment, the saloon was short two girls on her shift, and she would not be relieved from serving drinks for about another hour.

She hoped that the delay would not kill the agreement that they had made. She promised him a little extra for the delay, and Ed, wondering what "extra" she had in mind, agreed to wait.

§

Besides all of that, she said that I was cute. Now I have been called rugged or big or many other things, but never have I been called "cute!" Of course I agreed to wait the hour, and I gave her one large gold coin to seal the agreement. I took a parting look at her, and I was pleased, knowing that I had made a good deal.

I left the bar area and went into the large side room, where I saw lots of people sitting down in chairs so that they could listen to someone who was about to speak. I had looked at the advertisement on the board outside the room and decided that this would be a good way to spend the time waiting on Sunny to finish up at the bar.

The printed sign said that the speaker was someone named Nathan who was an up-close eyewitness to the hottest story going around the western states, about a gunfight that involved some very famous names. The gunfight that Nathan was going to talk about was now being called "the gunfight at the O.K. Corral."

I squeezed into a comer and waited patiently for Nathan to appear. I wanted to hear all about Wyatt Earp and Doc Holliday and all the goings-on at the O.K. Corral, but my mind was still stuck on those great-looking breasts of Sunny the bartender!

§

One of the two watchers who usually stood on the second level above the saloon floor passed out some paperwork that gave the background to what we were going to be hearing in a few minutes. I took the time to read it through. The paper read as follows:

October 26, 1881, Tombstone, Arizona, territory of the United States of America.

There was little that Nathan could do but watch as the feuding factions came together in a vacant lot between McDonald's assay office and C.S. Fly's lodging house. The vacant lot between the two buildings was the property of the O.K. Corral Company, which used the area to board some of the local horses that were used by the Wells Fargo stagecoach line.

Nathan, who worked as a clerk at the McDonald assay office, was sitting on the front porch smoking a cigar on his lunch hour, when all the gathering players started moving into the wide-open area of the corral. Nathan immediately left the porch and went up to the second floor and stood by the open window looking down on the scene. He was close enough to see everything clearly and to hear their voices. What he saw was two groups of cowboys standing about twenty feet from each other.

Nathan knew all of them on sight, having lived in Tombstone his whole life. The first group was made up of five men, two pairs of whom were brothers. They were the brothers Ike and Billy Clanton, the brothers McLaury, and Billy Clairborne, who was known as a gunfighter.

The other group of four that was facing them were United States Marshal Wyatt Earp and his two brothers, Virgil and Morgan Earp. Wyatt's friend, the famous Doc Holliday, who was also known as a gunfighter, was also there.

Nathan knew that there were bad feelings between the two groups, in that the first group of Clantons, Mclaury's, and Clairborne, were known to be cattle rustlers and highwaymen. He also knew that the second group had sworn to enforce the law and "stop their evil doings." Both groups had carefully avoided each other until they all came together at that moment when Nathan was physically there to witness the goings on.

Nathan saw that all four of the Earp group were wearing badges, and he assumed that Wyatt Earp, the marshal, had made them all his deputies for the round-up of the criminals that they were now about to face down. Everyone was armed with a six-shooter except for Tom McLaury, who stood behind his horse with a Winchester rifle on his saddle.

Nathan also noted that Doc Holliday, who was standing opposite Tom McLaury and his horse, had his pistol holstered at his side and was holding a sawed-off shot-gun in his right hand.

Wyatt Earp was the first to speak and Nathan heard the words loud and clear:

"All right, you sons of bitches, you've been looking for a fight, and now you can have it. Either drop your weapons right now, or come up shooting!"

"No!" shouted Ike Clanton. "Look. I'm not armed!" He opened up his coat and showed that he was not carrying a gun.

"Up with your hands, now!" was Virgil Earp's reply.

Then things started happening much too fast for Nathan to see what started the shooting. All at once, he saw Morgan Earp shoot Billy Clanton in the chest, while Wyatt, with a quick draw of his six-shooter, pumped three quick shots into Frank McLaury's stomach.

Wyatt Earp was yelling, "The fighting has now commenced! Fight or die!"

Doc Holliday fired both barrels of his shotgun directly into the other McLaury brother and then drew his six-shooter and began to fire. Billy Clanton, as he was falling with a fatal gunshot wound, fired two quick shots, one hitting Morgan Earp, and the other hitting Virgil Earp. Nathan thought that the entire shooting had taken less than sixty seconds, and could not believe his watch when he took the time to look at it.

The outcome of the shooting was both McLaury brothers and Billy Clanton dead, with the other two gunfighters wounded. Doc Holliday, Virgil Earp and Morgan Earp were slightly wounded and only needed minor medical attention.

Of all the nine men who took part in the shootout, only Wyatt Earp was unhurt. He later was heard saying it was because of his living such a clean life. Everyone who heard him say that laughed out loud, and the word went around that Wyatt always joined in the laughter himself.

The hero of our little written report, Nathan, got on his horse and took off for places far away. He was smart enough to realize that he was the only eyewitness to what happened, and he knew that if he gave testimony, one group or the other would kill him, depending on what he had to say.

Nathan has said that he will not be staying in the Arizona

territory tonight; that he will head off to California to stay with a sister. He is quoted as saying that he thought that leaving for good would be much better for his health. We wish Nathan well, and we hope you will enjoy listening to him as he talks about his personal and up-close eyewitness account in a few minutes.

Thank you for taking the time to read this article.

Sincerely,

The management

§

AUTHOR BUD'S SIDEBAR NOTES AND FOLLOW-UP TO THE FAMOUS GUNFIGHT AT THE O.K. CORRAL:

WITH REVENGE AS THE ABSOLUTE MOTIVE, THE FOLLOWING EVENTS WERE PUT IN MOTION AND HAPPENED SHORTLY THEREAFTER:

SIX MONTHS LATER, MORGAN EARP WAS PLAYING A GAME OF BILLARDS WITH HIS BROTHER WYATT, WHEN TWO MASKED MEN BURST IN AND FIRED AT THE TWO BROTHERS.

MORGAN EARP WAS KILLED BUT THE BULLET MEANT FOR WYATT COMPLETELY MISSED AND HE WENT ON WITH HIS LIFE.

2.THREE MONTHS AFTER MORGAN WAS KILLED, VIRGIL EARP WAS SHOT IN THE BACK WITH A SHOTGUN BLAST. HE DIED AT THE SCENE.

THE TERRITORY OF ARIZONA SURELY LOVED INDIVIDUAL GUNFIGHTS, AND THE GREATEST NUMBER OF FIGHTS TOOK PLACE, OF COURSE, IN TOMBSTONE.

AND NOW BACK TO OUR STORY OF BIG ED JOHNSON.

§

Big Ed decided not to stay and listen to Nathan's talk. The

papers that he had just read told him most of the story, and the few extra details that Nathan would probably add didn't matter to him.

Ed agreed that the best thing for Nathan to do was to get out of Arizona and just disappear. One group or the other would definitely be after him if he told about what he saw and heard.

Big Ed walked back into the saloon area, where he received a wave from Sunny, who was just taking off her apron and handing it to the new girl who was coming on duty.

It was simply amazing how much the back-up bartender looked like Sunny. The biggest difference, of course, was their hair color. Sunny was a blonde, and the other pretty lady had hair that was more into the brown shades.

Sunny pointed to a nearby table, and then pointed to the ladies' rest-room. She wanted to freshen up a bit.

When Sunny finally did come over and sit down, she brought with her a bottle of the house's finest whiskey and two glasses for them. She also said that she took the liberty of ordering them steaks for dinner. She said that she was starving because she wasn't able to take a break from the double shift that she had to work behind the bar.

Ed was pleased to share the bottle with her, and he also said that he was hungry. This would give him time to talk with Sunny and get to know who she really was, besides being a bargirl.

While Nathan's lecture was going on in the next room, they pretty much had the entire saloon area to themselves. The other bartenders, seeing that Sunny was with a paying customer, also left them alone. Dinner arrived, and their conversation was at a minimum as they each quickly put away the food that was placed before them.

Of course her real name was not Sunny. That was just the professional name that she used when she was working. He learned that her given name was Barbara Jean and that her friends called her Barb or Barbara. She was twenty-seven years old, and came from a family of four sisters. She was the second to the youngest. They had lost their parents to sickness many years ago, and they had to split up and each go their separate ways in order to survive.

She found herself to be good at bartending, and since they allowed her to do sexual encounters whenever she wanted, she found herself making a good living. The deal that she made with the establishment was that she had to split her tips for services rendered, on a fifty/fifty basis, and that was why her fees were so high.

This made a lot of good sense to Ed, who knew all about doing whatever was needed to survive.

Her plans were to find the man of her dreams, get married and raise lots of kids. She thought that since she was so good at getting along with people, that her future might be in owning a dress shop or a small dry-goods store somewhere in a small town. She loved Arizona, where the weather was usually very pleasant, and the people she came in contact with were more considerate that elsewhere.

Originally her family was from Kentucky, which gave Ed something to talk about, since he was from the next state over, which was Tennessee, and he often went hunting with his brothers in Kentucky. They seemed to really enjoy talking to each other, but when they finally ran out of small talk, Sunny excused herself, and said that she wanted to make herself more presentable for him.

She gave him a key to the room she had reserved for the night. It was on the second floor toward the rear of the long hallway. The room number was 234.

Big Ed sat there and watched her as she walked off toward the stairway that led upstairs to their room. He was hoping that, beyond the great sex that he was looking forward to, they could possibly be friends beyond all of this. She seemed to be the type of girl that he was always looking for. She was smart, beautiful, resourceful and she said that he was "cute!"

He waited the proper amount of time, used the men's room off of the saloon floor, and then walked up the stairs that led to room 234.

§

At the feel of her hands on him, Ed wrapped his arms around her and drew her against him. It was heaven feeling her warm, feminine body pressed against him.

Her hands glided up to his cheeks, cupping them gently in her palms. She tipped her head up and gazed into his eyes with what he took for an internal longing of some sort, and that look of hers simply accelerated his own heartbeat.

She settled her mouth on his with gentle precision, while her arms slid around his neck and her lips moved under his lips, which were soft and giving. Her tongue speared gently into his mouth, and he murmured his approval.

He pulled her tighter to his body, feeling a tide of desire wash through him. Her magnificent breasts pressed against his chest as he felt his excitement growing by leaps and bounds. His groin tightened in direct response to her, and he felt himself beginning to expand his manhood. He knew that he was responding to her far too quickly.

With all of his self-discipline, his experience, and his willpower, he should have been able to delay a final erection for hours. And yet this special woman had him hungering for her even in the few minutes that they have been together.

He knew that he would be thinking about all of this once he got back into the saddle and continued on his way west. He had not expected this to happen so fast. She was simply overwhelming him with her beauty and her willingness to be had by him.

Her soft sounds quivered their way through him. She snuggled closer, her hands gliding down his chest, then around his waist and finally cupping his buttocks.

His fingers caressed along the low neckline of her blouse, then dipped into the fabric in order to release the first button that held it together. He released the next button, then the next, thrilling her senses with his absolutely delicate touch. She did not expect a man as big as Big Ed to be so tender and careful. Finally her blouse gaped open, and he lifted it over her shoulders and dropped it to the floor.

He stroked gently along the edge of her bra, then between her breasts. He released the front clasp and reverently drew the restraining cups aside. The look of awe on his face nearly melted her heart. He was so very sensitive, and she was rapidly learning to appreciate him.

"You are exquisite!" he exclaimed.

His heated gaze took in her breasts, and her nipples puckered shamelessly. She longed for him to touch them, but he did not. He merely took in the sight of them as he finally unfastened the rest of her outfit and slid it down her hips.

She stepped out of them, now wearing only her pink ankle socks and skimpy black panties. He hooked his fingers under the lace, and drew them down, then off.

Now naked, except for her little pink socks, she felt alluring and yet somehow innocent. He seemed to bring out these good feelings within her, and she liked what she was seeing in this most interesting man who called himself Big Ed. He gazed down at the socks and smiled, as if he was having the same thoughts.

She took his hand and led him across the living room and into that section that was acting as the bedroom. The king-sized bed seemed appropriate for him. When a guy was this big he needed a big bed to do his thing in!

She rolled the navy and forest green covers down to reveal cream-colored sheets and pillowcases with a fancy navy ribbon edging around them.

She sat down, and the high-quality cotton sheets felt like silk against her naked skin.

Ed tossed aside two of the pillows and moved the remaining two to the center of the bed. "Why don't you lie on your stomach, Sunny?" he suggested.

She settled onto her stomach, tucking one pillow under her chin and pushing the other aside.

He sat down beside her, and his hands began moving over her back in long soothing strokes. Relaxing, rhythmic circles … up the center of her back, across her shoulders, then down to her hips … then up the center once again.

She found herself relaxing under his sure touch. She thought that she was supposed to be giving him pleasure, but here he was doing wonderful things to her instead. It must make him happy touching her, and she was happy being touched in such a remarkable fashion.

He rolled her over onto her side, and moved her hands over her head. With one hand he held her hands while they were still up above her head. With his free hand, he wandered over her well-formed and very firm breasts. This was what he had been waiting for! His hand moved from one nipple to the other. To Big Ed, this special touching was well worth the high price that he had to pay for the use of this willing female body. He was a very happy man!

Big Ed felt himself growing hard again. He was always a breast man and this girl had the ultimate set. He was having one of the best times of his life as he pulled her flat onto her back once again. As she rolled back and he released her hands, he grasped the pillow and repositioned it under her head.

She just lay there, staring up at him, her body simply beautiful in its nakedness. Her breasts pointed straight up to the ceiling, the nipples were fully erect. Her soft golden pubic hair curled daintily between her thighs as her long legs parted in anticipation of his entry.

He eased her legs further apart, and carefully positioned himself between them. He gently drew the folds leading to her woman-hood apart, and dabbed his tongue against the tender flesh that led into her inner chamber.

Sunny's fingers tangled in his hair, and she moaned in pleasure from what he was beginning to do to her.

He took a moment and lifted his head and just gazed at her. She looked beautiful to him, and he gave the biggest of sighs, and then nudged her thighs wider apart as the sweet smell of her urged him on in an intoxicating series of moves. His eyes closed as his head went back, and he sucked in a lungful of air. The engorged and swollen head of his huge erection pierced and at last entered the young lady.

This was his moment. It was what he had been ready for since he first saw her moving about in the downstairs bar serving drinks. This was his special moment. He thought that this was probably the highlight of his sexual life. He had never had a woman such as Sunny and he was enjoying every single and glorious moment of it.

He pushed himself up onto his elbows, and with his eyes closed he drilled deeper and deeper into the depths of what made her a female. He was glorified by the feeling that the heavenly sliding of her body beneath him gave to him.

He never wanted this moment to end but he knew that it would. All good and wonderful things always came to an end, and this experience was no exception, with the fire within him raging to get loose. His need for release was too much for him, and as he was coming to his completion, he felt her getting caught up in that special moment with him. Sunny began to rock back and forth as she matched his pounding motions with her own strong body.

And finally, he stroked one final, mind-blowing stroke, and completed his act! He was immediately followed by Sunny who screamed out loud with the ultimate pleasure that Ed had just given her. It was the best screw that she had ever had, and she let out a scream of pleasure that she was sure came from her toes on up to her head!

They both lay there panting next to each other and just

looking into each other's eyes. This was a special moment that they shared with each other, and nothing could ever take away the memory of it for either of them for the rest of their lives.

Within moments, they both fell into a wonderfully deep sleep, completely entwined within each other's arms. The night sounds around them were completely ignored as they slept on.

§

It was possibly three or four hours later, when Sunny was awakened by Big Ed's hands, which were gently moving around her breasts. Big Ed felt the now-familiar rise of her nipples under his touch, and knew that she was ready for the next round of his love-making. Not a word was spoken between them as he gently but firmly rolled her over onto her stomach.

The woman was obviously well trained, as she immediately took up the proper position of putting her weight on her forward leaning arms, and lifting up her rear end, with her legs nicely spread out and waiting for him to enter. The bright moonlight coming in through the window showed him a special picture that he was sure that he would never forget.

Here was a fabulous female, on her hands and knees, with a great set of breasts hanging down, just waiting for him to fondle them. She was starting to make some up-and-down motions in anticipation of his entering her from the rear, but he was in no hurry to do so. Moments like these were few and far between, and he wanted to drag them out for as long as he could.

He ran his hands over her swaying butt, and around those marvelous breasts, and was enjoying himself tremendously until his own erection got in his way. He knew that it was time to finish off his love-making in what was his favorite way of doing so. He reached forward and played with her breasts for the last time. He would really miss them!

He already was making plans in his head to come back and visit Sunny again, once he settled into his job with the United

States Marshal's office in Phoenix.

Big Ed, of course, was a breast man as are most males. He gave that great twosome one last squeeze and then entered her from the rear. He heard her gasp as his huge erection went just where it belonged. She would remember for a long time why Big Ed was called Big Ed!

He continued to pump into this willing woman, going deeper and deeper until he was in as far as he could go. He felt her expanding and stretching inside to take in all of him.

Minutes later, he was completely done, and he climbed off and held Sunny one last time as they again spoke no words, and once again fell asleep in each other's arms. These were special moments that both of them would long remember.

ALEXANDER THE GREAT

THIS NEXT SHORT STORY IS A LITTLE DIFFERENT.

IT IS A BRIEF ACCOUNT OF THE UNBELIEVABLE CONNECTION BETWEEN ALEXANDER THE GREAT, THE WORLD CONQUERER, AND CLEOPATRA, THE BEAUTIFUL QUEEN OF EGYPT.

THE MOST INTERESTING PART OF THIS ACCURATE HISTORICAL ACCOUNT, IS THAT THE TWO MAIN FIGURES IN THE STORY LIVED SOME TWELVE (12) GENERATIONS APART!

AND YET THEIR LIVES ARE DEFINITELY CONNECTED IN A MOST INTERESTING WAY (TODAY'S LAS VEGAS, NEVADA, CAN LEARN A THING OR TWO FROM THE TWIST IN THIS TRUE STORY).

A SHORT, VERY TWISTED AND FINALLY PASSIONATE HISTORICAL SHORT STORY BY BUD SELIGSON

§

THE YEAR IS 334 BCE.

At the battle of the Granius River in northwestern Eurasia, during the very first military engagement of Alexander the Great' s invasion of the Persian Empire, young King Alexander came very close to a sudden death.

At the Granius River, Alexander's Greeks encountered the

enemy Persians on the opposite bank. The enemy was greatly massed in a purely defensive formation and did not seem ready for a fight.

The young King Alexander, age twenty-two, obviously had much to learn. He did not listen to his senior commanders who cautioned him to stand down and wait for his reinforcements that were due to arrive the next day.

Ignoring their sensible advice, Alexander mounted his great horse Bucephalus. He was wearing a white-plumed helmet, which made him stand out from everyone else, because they all were wearing dark helmets. The young King led his shock cavalry troops in an audacious charge across the river and up the opposite bank.

The Persian forces fell back before the attacking Greeks, and King Alexander, who did not stop his charge, suddenly found himself in the middle of the enemy lines. This was probably exactly what the Persian tacticians had planned from the beginning. Due to the suddenness of his unwise charge right into the very middle of the enemy lines, he only had with him a very small number of his men. The rest were momentarily cut off from the main body of the Greeks, whose mounted cavalry were trying to catch up.

At this critical moment in the battle, young Alexander was completely surrounded by enemies, including one Spithridates, an ax-wielding Persian noble, who managed to deal Alexander a heavy blow to his head. Alexander's helmet was severely damaged and the King was disoriented and unable to defend himself. A second blow would certainly kill him, and with the young King would die the hopes of the entire expedition, and all the Greek imperial aspirations.

Greece would never have risen to greatness as it did if Alexander had died, and the entire world as we know it would have been changed forever. In those next few seconds, the future of the Great Persian Empire, and the entire course of Western European history would be decided.

Did Alexander's brief life flash before him as he awaited imminent extinction? How had he come to arrive at this place and at this terrible fate that was to befall him within seconds? How could so much have come to depend on a single blow to the head?

§

Alexander was born in Macedon (which is a northeastern region of modem Greece) in the year 356 BCE. He was the first and only son of King Philip the Second of Macedon.

King Philip had seized control of Macedon just three years before his son's birth. By the time Alexander was ten years old, Macedon was the most powerful state on the entire Greek Peninsula. Alexander was being groomed to help govern the kingdom, and eventually assume the throne of his father.

Alexander was being well trained! His tutor in intellectual and cultural matters was with the world-famous and most brilliant Greek philosopher, Aristole. His mentor in military and diplomatic affairs was his own father, who was probably the best military mind of his entire generation. And in the corridors of the Royal Palace, Alexander learned the dark art of political intrigue. The Greek Court was always full of rumor and lying factions.

§

In Alexander's twentieth year, King Philip was cut down by an assassin. The killer was another Greek named Pausanias, who was immediately killed by King Philip's personal guards after the deed was done. He was killed as he ran out of the palace trying to escape on his waiting horse.

Although Pausanias may well have held a personal grudge against King Philip for one reason or another, there was suspicion that he had not acted on his own. One obvious candidate for the mastermind behind the killing of King Philip was Darius III, the Great Enemy, King of all of Persia.

In the mid-fourth century, Persia was a mighty empire that stretched from the Aegean coast of Turkey to Egypt in the South, and went East as far as modem Pakistan. In the years before his assassination, King Philip had been making open preparations for a Persian expedition. A few months before his murder, his generals had established an army beachhead on Persian-held territory.

King Darrius of Persia was famous for his statements of always wanting to cut off the head of primary enemies whenever possible. This made him the prime and most hated of enemies. Alexander himself said in one of his public speeches that he personally blamed King Darius as the number-one suspect in the death of his father.

Other high-ranking Greek officials were pointing out that another prime suspect had to be the King's unstable and always jealous wife, Olympias (Alexander's mother).

Other people who had Alexander's ear at the Royal Court said that there were whispers going around in the shadows that the young Prince Alexander himself was somehow involved in the affair.

The kingdom was full of speculations as young Alexander took over the reins of government. He quickly assumed the full title of King of all Greece, and there was no one who officially opposed him. But there was plenty of whispering going on behind his back.

Alexander had definitely proven himself ready and more than worthy to rightfully take his father's empty throne. His biggest problem was that the old King had invested heavily in getting his huge army ready to invade Persia, and the Royal Treasury was seriously depleted. Whether or not he wanted to invade Persia using his father's plans was not an option for Alexander.

He stepped right in and continued with the plans to invade

the closest provinces of the great Persian Empire. He held out the prospect of great war treasures that were there for the taking, and he was able to fire up the imaginations of his Greek troops.

And now that brings us to where the ax of the Persian soldier was getting ready to strike the shattered helmet of young King Alexander for the second time. It appeared as if the great and glorious expedition would end right there at the very first battle before things really got started. Yet the deadly blow never was delivered, nor even given.

Just as the Persian soldier Spithridates prepared to finish off the King, one of Alexander's personal bodyguards (nick-named Cleitus the Black), appeared at his king's side and speared the Persian nobleman dead on the spot. Alexander quickly rallied his soldiers and, in a wild charge that might have ended in disaster, spurred on his troops to victory. Most of the enemy forces crumbled before Alexander as the battles raged on for many days.

Alexander was spectacularly victorious! He lost only thirty-four men, and killed over twenty thousand of the enemy. These numbers were so impressive that thousands of more homeland Greeek soldiers rushed from their homes to join him in his battles. There is nothing that brings success like success itself!

Great amounts of treasure and the spoils of the war against the Persians were sent back to Greece to be displayed in places of honor. The sight of so much treasure that was to be divided up with every single soldier who joined the army soon gave Alexander an overwhelming force of men at arms. Alexander was now on his way up, and it seemed that nothing could slow him down.

In the course of the next ten years, Alexander and his Greek army repeatedly demonstrated their capacity to overcome tremendous odds. Alexander went on to conquer the entire Persian Empire and much more. Historians have stated over and over that Alexander's conquest of the great Persian Empire was among the most remarkable military campaigns of all time.

Alexander had placed his name in the history books as one of the all-time greatest generals that ever took up arms.

By 324 BCE, Alexander had laid the foundation for a successful empire that might have included over one-half of the known world at that time. And here is where we must understand why Alexander's conquest of the rest of the known world never happened. Unfortunately, Alexander did not live long enough to see his hard-fought new empire get started.

In the year 324 BCE, Alexander the Great, king of Greece, ruled a domain that stretched from Egypt to the distant Caspian Sea. Historians call him over and over again one of the most brilliant soldiers of all time. Sadly enough, he did not die a warrior's death in battle, but expired as helpless as a baby in his own bed.

On the night of June 1, 323 BCE, within the royal bedchambers of his palace in Babylon, Alexander was holding a memorial feast to honor a personal friend. Suddenly, around mid-evening, he was seized with intense pain and collapsed.

He was taken to his bedchambers, where he tried to fight off a raging fever. He came back and forth into awareness but finally passed on after ten days of intense suffering.

The passing of Alexander the Great is one of history's most enduring mysteries. What caused the strong and healthy young ruler to so quickly and unexpectedly die at the very height of his power? Historians have proposed malaria, typhoid, and alcohol poisoning as possible causes of death. There has never been an investigation into any of these possibilities.

CLEOPATRA

And now, here is the link that connects Cleopatra of Egypt to the dying Alexander the Great hundreds of years later!

Please recall that in the last few days of his life, Alexander came in and out of his fever. In one of his few moments of clarity, he had his doctors send for his four most senior army generals.

When they finally all appeared before him in one of those moments when he was alert and clear thinking, he told them that he had not been prepared for his own death at so young an age. He told them that he had not thought about who should step into his shoes and become the next leader of the world that he created. He said that he was sorry, but no young man ever thinks about his own death.

Rather than have the four of them fight against each other and tear the new empire apart, he divided up the empire into four parts. Each one of these four generals was to get one part of the empire as his very own to rule as they saw fit. They had to each take an oath before him now, to support each other in their new positions and come to the aid of each other in case of need.

Alexander then had one of his loyal servants bring in a hand drawn map of the newly formed Empire. In bright red, there were four large sections drawn. One was Europe, one was Asia, one was Greece, and the last was Egypt.

Alexander said that in his opinion, each area was worthy of any of them, but he ranked the greatest prizes in the following order: Greece, Asia, Europe, Egypt. He said that it would become clear in a few moments which part of the Empire would belong to each of them.

Again the servant came in, but this time he was carrying a large wooden box that had wooden walls built up on three sides of it. The servant set down a pair of large dice in the very center of the wooden three-sided box.

Alexander said that each of the four generals would roll the pair of dice, and the highest number rolled by the generals would get the best area, and so on down to the fourth choice as per the list he had drawn up. He again told them that any of the four areas would be extremely valuable, of course, and they should not feel badly if the luck of the dice gave them a lower position. They would roll alphabetically according to their last names: General Cassander, General Lysimachus, General Ptolemy, and finally General Selencus.

After much mumbling and complaining, the four generals got down on their knees and prepared to roll the dice that would divide up the known world.

The servant wrote each name on a scroll and was prepared to write down the number each general would roll with the dice.

Alexander had himself placed in a soft chair next to the kneeling generals so that he could watch up close, this most unusual of events.

General Cassander rolled a six and a three for a total of nine. The number nine was entered next to his name.

General Lysimachus rolled a six and a five for a total of eleven. The number eleven was entered by the servant next to his name.

General Ptolemy rolled a three and a one for a total of four. The number four was entered next to his name.

General Selencus rolled a six and a five for a total of eleven. The number eleven was entered by the servant next to his name.

The servant cleared his throat and read, "Generals

Lysimachus and General Selencus will have to roll the dice one more time. They have tied with the number eleven, and since they are the two top numbers, they will get the top two selections."

The servant continued, "General Cassander rolled a nine which makes him the third highest number, and he receives Europe. Congratulations, General."

"General Ptolemy rolled a number four which makes him the fourth highest number, and he receives Egypt. Congratulations, General.

"And now, Generals Lysimachus and Selencus, roll the dice one more time each. Alphabetically, if you please! Kindly allow General Lysimachus to roll first.

The General's dice rolled a pair of fives for a total of ten.

General Selencus's dice rolled a six and a one for a total of seven.

The servant announced, "General Lysimachus rolled the high number, and he receives Greece. Congratulations, General.

"General Selencus comes in second and he receives Asia. Congratulations, General."

The four generals were now gathered around the seated Alexander, who was absolutely exhausted.

Alexander was saying, "You have all been with me from the very beginning. Words are not adequate for what I feel in my heart for each of you. The best gift that I can give each of you is one-quarter of the Empire that we all worked so hard to create. I wish you all the very best of everything that life can give you. Please remember me as I was, and not as I am at this moment." He waved his hand, and each general bowed and quietly left the room.

Alexander passed away quietly in the night, and the great man was gone for all eternity.

§

And now, here is the kicker that I promised you.

General Ptolemy came in fourth in the dice roll, but he became the real winner of all this, because all of the other three generals were overthrown as rulers of the countries they had won and were put to death. Only the fourth-place winner and biggest loser overall in the dice-throwing contest, General Ptolemy, established a dynasty that lasted.

His family ruled Egypt for thirteen generations in his direct line until Cleopatra and her brother Ptolemy the thirteenth took over as co-rulers of the Egyptian empire at a time when Julius Caesar, Mark Antony and other interesting Romans that we shall read about in the next few pages were rising around them.

For me, the most interesting result of all of this was that the world was divided up into what still exists today in our own world as a result of a losing pair of dice being thrown in a game of chance! Las Vegas can never top this one as the biggest roll of the dice at a gambling event ever held.

§

The story of Cleopatra, the last Queen of Egypt, does not start and end with her. The story of Egypt itself is worth noting because it was so very important to the ancient world.

Please remember that we are talking about civilizations that were at the very top of their games over twenty-four hundred years ago. The importance of Egypt has always been due to the overflowing Nile River, which gave a great abundance of food crops to the world. In those ancient times, whoever controlled Egypt also controlled what was known as the bread basket of the Ancient World.

§

Cleopatra was born in the year 69 BCE and died in the year 30 BCE at the young age of thirty-nine.

She was the eldest child of Ptolemy the Twelfth, who died in a hunting accident. He left two children to take over his vacant throne. Cleopatra was just nineteen and her younger brother was twelve. As was the custom, they married each other, but were both extremely unhappy with the marriage.

Cleopatra, with her extremely strong personality, set herself up as the main ruler of Egypt, and just pushed her younger brother aside. The twelve-year-old Ptolemy was unhappy at being pushed aside, and with the help of his personal advisors, declared Cleopatra an outlaw and put to death any and all persons who dared to aid her.

Cleopatra was forced to flee from the palace, and took with her hundreds of personal and loyal followers. Cleopatra fled to the countryside, where she raised an army that was able to hold off the army of her brother when they came after her. They finally settled into an uneasy truce that left Ptolemy inside the royal palace and Cleopatra in control of the surrounding countryside.

Now entering the picture came Julius Caesar of Rome. He came to Egypt to personally set up an agreement to buy all the food supplies that he needed for his huge army that was expanding Roman influence through the area.

When the great Caesar learned of the split between the royal siblings, he declared himself neutral, and said that he would only deal with whoever had the power to sell him the supplies he needed. That someone turned out to be Cleopatra's brother, and Caesar moved his headquarters into one of the empty palace rooms so as to be near the seller of the goods he needed.

And here is the interesting point of this fascinating and true story. Cleopatra up to that moment, had never met Julius Caesar in person. Whenever food items were sold from the countryside that she controlled, she always would deal with one of Caesar's officers who told her that the great Caesar rarely if ever would leave the comforts of the palace. Cleopatra absorbed this bit of knowledge into the plan that she was forming.

Now, let us talk about Cleopatra herself for a moment. Not only was she said to be a beautiful young woman who was nineteen years old and reportedly very intelligent, but it was said that she was able to speak nine different languages with no accent at all. It seems that she learned the languages from the few buyers who would come out to the countryside to buy some of her food products.

Now, Cleopatra was smart enough to know that she could not win the civil war that she was involved in against her younger brother, so she came up with a plan that would allow her to meet with Julius Caesar in person.

She was well aware that Caesar had stationed outside of the city, his standing army which was about double the size of her small number of soldiers, and those of her brother's (husband's, if you wish). She came up with the clever pretense of having a group of local merchants deliver and install carpeting into several of the rooms inside the palace.

The palace rooms were known to be cold and drafty, and no one questioned the carpet installers as they went about their work. After a few days, when the installers were now well-known to the guards who surrounded Julius Caesar, she put her plan into action!

It was early the next morning when we find the practically naked and perfectly beautiful nineteen-year-old Cleopatra being dressed by several of her maids in front of a tall standing mirror.

Her hair is black, and she is wearing it up in what we would call a bun. A holding clip of some sort is holding her long hair in place. We assume that she is wearing it up so that when she is rolled up and into the large rug that her plan calls for, she can possibly see out of the corner of her eye with no hair getting in her way.

She has an extreme amount of makeup on her face, which is normal for this time period. There is a lot of purple and black shading around her eyes which gives them an appearance of being bigger than they really are.

Let us take a moment here and talk about Cleopatra's nose! Historians have said that they thought it had a hook and a funny look about it. Historically speaking, I have to disagree with them. Right now, at nineteen, she had what would be called a pug nose, which to my understanding is a small nose that is a bit wide but is rather cute.

Her makeup does not cover the many freckles that are all over her face. These are there because she is so young, and they will probably disappear in the next few years.

Her speaking voice is what we could call husky. It is somewhat deep and yet sweet and melodic as she calls out her instructions to her maids.

One cannot help but notice the ease and smoothness of her movements as she carefully puts on her earrings. Her ears are pierced, just as girls have been doing for centuries. This seems to tie females together in one big 'girls' club' since the earliest of civilized times. The actual earrings look like twisted brooches made out of silver and are in the form of flowers. They are quite attractive on her.

One of the maids comes up behind Cleopatra and secures a fine, well-made, tiny golden crown on the back of her head. This was probably put in place so as not to leave any doubt in Caesar's mind that he was in the presence of a queen of the royal bloodline. Around her soft throat was a lovely diamond necklace. She was now wearing more jewelry than she was clothing.

She practiced fluttering her eyes, which would dance behind her long lashes as she fluttered them. The stories about her remarkable beauty were not overstated. This is one beautiful young woman and Julius Caesar is in for one great big surprise if she can get herself into his room with no one else present.

One of the maids helped her on with a splendid robe which shone with the brightness of fire. It was basically golden with all styles of needlework embroidered into it, and it shimmered like the moon on a bright night.

Cleopatra was just about ready for her command performance! Julius Caesar was about to discover an exotic female, full of grace and beauty. And a female who definitely had plans.

She told the maid, who had by now set down the full-length mirror, to step outside and ask the three workmen who were waiting there to please enter. There followed a few minutes of conversation before the three men acknowledged that they understood the queen's instructions. Each man had a very large smile on his face when she handed each of them a very large-sized money pouch that was packed with gold pieces.

Cleopatra was a smart one. She overpaid the three workers to be sure that they would do exactly what she instructed them to do. She was trying to make sure that there were no mistakes. She had only this one opportunity to get at Julius Caesar and everything had to work perfectly. She had dismissed her maids so that they would not be able to listen in on her conversation with the workmen.

All was in readiness as the workers started to spread out the huge rug in the middle of the room.

§

We shall never know what was racing though Cleopatra's mind as she was being carried down the main hallway on her way to the sleeping quarters of Caesar. She was unhappy about the roughness with which she was being carried by the workers she had hired. She felt that they were carrying her along as if she were an expensive sack of potatoes!

The walking finally stopped as the lead worker knocked heavily on the door, and a booming voice answered, "Come in." The unseen voice spoke Egyptian with a heavy accent, and everyone knew that this was the voice of Julius Caesar.

The lead man led the men in and quickly took a look around the room. Within a few moments, he felt assured that the great Caesar was completely alone. He pointed to the ground, and the other two workers carefully set their burden down and walked rapidly out of the room.

Caesar had not yet looked up from whatever it was that he was working on.

The lead worker stepped over to the top of the carpet, took a firm hold of it, and said the nine famous words that he had been taught to say. "Great Caesar! Here is something very special for you." Without another moment's hesitation, he quickly unrolled the carpet, which caused Cleopatra to spin around as the carpet finally lay open on the flat floor.

It was only a few moments until Cleopatra was helped to her feet by the worker, who quickly bowed to the general, and then again to his queen. He fled from the room and snapped the door shut behind him.

Cleopatra was dizzy for a moment from the spin on the floor, but the spunky nineteen-year-old took just a moment to recover. She took a few small steps forward toward the open-mouthed Caesar, and dropped her covering gown on the floor behind her. There was not one word spoken between the two of them as she did a deep bow of respect before the great Caesar, and then straightened up to her full height, and stood there defiantly, with her snow-white breasts stretching out before her.

It was obvious that Julius Caesar, ruler of the greatest empire that the world had known up to that time, had fallen under Cleopatra's spell the moment he had put his eyes on her. It must be remembered that even though he was the great leader, Julius Caesar was still a man.

The room was so quiet, that if you listened carefully you could hear a pin drop. Well, that pin would have been thunderous if it had fallen, because without a word, Caesar, the only man in the room, put down his papers and walked over to the standing Cleopatra, where he slowly made a complete circle around her. It was like he was buying a new horse at an auction, and he was checking out her conformation.

Still not a word was spoken as he came around to the front once again, bowed deeply to show his respect for Cleopatra, and then reached for and gently took her left arm in his right, and slowly led her over to the far end of the room where he had his small sleeping bed.

She smiled at him and he smiled at her as he slowly and gently removed the few bits of clothing that she had on. He did it quite slowly, and by the smile that was on his face, seemed to be really enjoying himself. He touched as little of her body as he could while removing the bits of remaining clothing.

It was only a few moments later that Cleopatra, still not having said a word in any of the nine languages that she knew, was lying flat on her back looking up at Caesar. Her eyes then followed him as he slowly walked across the room and secured the lock on the door. Obviously, he realized that this was not a good time to be interrupted.

Her eyes continued to watch him as he rapidly removed his sword belt, and the three or four other weapons that he had secured about his body. He seemed pretty sure that Cleopatra had no concealed weapons on her.

§

Shortly we find that Julius Caesar has replaced Cleopatra on the bed, where he was now lying flat on his back with his slightly hooded eyes open wide, somewhat glazed with excitement and ecstasy. He was breathing heavily, his arms extended at his sides. His restrained body was bucking wildly as he tried to futilely lift his head from the satin sheathed pillow, then let it fall back. He moaned loudly.

Caesar was a much older man than the young Cleopatra, who had just mounted him moments ago. He was still a robust and energetic man, with a stocky build and an expressive face that displayed a full range of expressions from stinging pain to indescribable pleasure—all in a matter of a few seconds. Naturally, the source of both the pain and the pleasure was Cleopatra, queen of the Nile, who was straddling him.

She was less than half his age, dazzlingly beautiful, with classic features and a magnificently sculpted muscular young body. It was a body topped by black waves of curls that had flown out of the holding comb that was supposed to be holding her hair back, but now flowed loosely above her smooth shoulders.

Her voluptuous high breasts jiggled provocatively as she straddled her new lover with her hips grinding into his pelvis and her bare buttocks smacking loudly against his outstretched legs.

Suddenly she slapped his thigh hard, eliciting another moan from the older, heavy-breathing man. Then she slapped his other thigh, the blow much more powerful, the force of it leaving a red impression on Caesar's chalky white skin. Again, he moaned, utterly lost in the strangely harmonious confluence of the pleasure and the pain.

Cleopatra closed her eyes, threw her head back, and thrust her breasts forward as Caesar fondled them and pinched her taut nipples. Slowly her head came forward, and her long-lashed eyes opened wide. A great smile exposed her bright and perfect white teeth.

It was obvious that Cleopatra was rapturously enthralled, not only with the very act of sex, but with being in complete control of everything that was taking place around her. She was setting the pace with this man, controlling the activity of their movements, and determining who did what to whom, and she was loving it!

Caesar moaned again, then noisily sucked in another mouthful of precious air. The woman leaned forward with one nipple gently brushing against his lip. As his head rose again from the pillow, she quickly raised her body, and moved her tantalizing breasts just out of reach. Caesar was whimpering like a child!

Now she was sitting straight up on him, rocking again, harder this time. Her head was turning from side to side as she steadily increased the tempo.

Both lovers were bathed in sweat, and their skin seemed to glow in the subdued light that was allowed to come into the room from the narrow high windows. The rocking continued, the sound of skin slapping skin reverberating throughout the large room. This was a sound interspersed with moans of pleasure from both lovers.

Caesar grunted, then gasped again and again as the woman responded to him by reaching down and gripping his hips, jerked them upward demandingly, forcing him deeper and deeper inside her.

Caesar issued a long low wail that seemed to build as the woman on top of him again increased the pace of their lovemaking up another notch.

And then finally it was over.

§

Hours later found Julius Caesar and Queen Cleopatra talking quietly in his command tent, which was in the center of his army that had settled on the outskirts of the city.

They talked about many things, and Caesar was satisfied that he alone would get all the foodstocks that he needed for his army, and Cleopatra agreed to be his lover whenever he had the time to leave Rome and visit with her.

Cleopatra was happy that Caesar agreed to arrest her brother Ptolemy and put him to death within the next forty-eight hours.

Her brother's small army would be added to Cleopatra's army, and together she would end up with a strong enough

Egyptian army that would be able to dominate all her surrounding small neighboring countries.

Cleopatra became the strongest leader for her region, and only Caesar's powerful city of Rome could control her.

§

After that hot and heavy love scene with Cleopatra and Julius Caesar, I'd like to step away from passion for a while and deal with just Julius Caesar., and the way he met his violent death by the hands of others.

Most people know that many years after he installed Cleopatra in Egypt, he was assassinated inside the Roman Senate.

I have always had four questions that bothered me about this terrible death that he was given and how easy it would have been for him to avoid it. I always thought that had Caesar lived, the Roman world would have continued expanding, and history would have come out different from the way it did.

Perhaps we would now be living in a better world—or maybe not.

Anyway, here are my four questions, and I of course did the research and also provide the correct historical answer to each of my questions as follows!

§

Question one: when Caesar left his army base on the day that he was going to attend a meeting at the Senate building, why did he not take his usual six-man security team with him?

Question two: when Caesar was driven in his usual horse-drawn chariot to the Senate building, why didn't the driver go in with him to fill out the usual six-man security team that he always had surrounding himself?

Question three: why did Caesar completely forgive one

of his biggest enemies, Brutus? It was Brutus who was the ringleader of the assassination that killed him. It was not in Caesar's character to overlook a former enemy and let Brutus walk all over the city as a free man, as he did.

Question four: when Caesar made his way to the special section that he had made for himself at the top of the Senate, why did he not notice that the regular guards who always encircled the entire Senate were missing?

The answers to the above questions will be found within the following short story.

§

It was quiet in the tent for a few minutes as Caesar was waiting for all of his officers to assemble.

Caesar's Roman legion of soldiers was at full strength when it was made up of no less than five thousand fighting men. Caesar's legions were made up only of Roman citizens; no outsiders were allowed to serve as soldiers.

Caesar made one concession to soldiers who were not Italian and wanted to join the Roman legions. He would require them to apply to become Roman citizens, and the treasure that he shared with his men would be held back from the non-Italians until they finished up their committed enlistment time. With gold, silver and other spoils of war waiting for them at the end of their enlistments, these foreign soldiers were always very loyal to their adopted country because they knew that there was a big payday waiting for them. Caesar always had great loyalty from all of his enlisted soldiers, whether Roman citizens or others.

Caesar did limit the foreign countries from which he would allow soldiers to join his legion. The surrounding countries of France, Germany and Belgium, were allowed to send their men to him. Caesar lumped the three countries' soldiers under one legion's banner and he called it the Legion from Gaul. In honor of Caesar, the term Gaul stuck to the three countries, and they were hereafter referred to under the cover-all term of Gaul.

These foreign enlistees had to stay in the army for five years before moving up to full citizenship. Roman and other Italian legionaries only had to serve three years.

There were dozens of existing legions, kept completely separated from one another, but they were all united under the general of the army, Julius Caesar, who paid their wages out of his own pocket. In this way, Caesar always had one hundred percent control of the armed forces for all of Italy.

It also goes without saying that Julius Caesar was a very rich man, and could easily afford the huge expense. History tells us that Caesar kept fifty percent of all valuable items such as gold, silver, weapons and fine jewelry that were taken from areas that his Roman legions conquered and then stripped of all movable assets. When in the later years of his life his Roman Legions overran areas of the countries now called Gaul, it was said that the riches that he pulled out of the country were beyond belief.

It has also been said time and time again in the history books that Julius Caesar had absolutely no mercy in his soul. It was also said that he ordered the slaughter of conquered armies down to the very last man in order to prevent them from rising up against Rome at another time. He was ruthless and had a real killer instinct, but his way of doing things was very successful for himself and for the city of Rome, which received the other fifty percent of his captured wealth.

All Roman soldiers had to provide their own weapons, which consisted of three long knives, two large broadswords, two regular swords, heavy metal armor, light metal armor, and armored helmets. Caesar would advance the soldiers the gold to buy the weapons they needed to join his armies, and then take the cost out of the monthly money they earned. It was said that he did not make a profit out of the sale of military equipment to his men, but what he got in return was the strength and absolute loyalty of the fighting forces of the powerful Roman legions.

To keep track of who owed money to him, Caesar had full time bookkeepers, as well as medical staff, engineers, and other specialty occupations such as priests and musicians who would also play marching songs when the troops went into battle.

One important item that history has pointed out about the Roman legions under Caesar leadership was the famous broadsword that he had specially made up for his legions. This broadsword was the ultimate weapon of the time, and when Caesar sent out one of his legions of five thousand men carrying this weapon in hand, no enemy could stand up against the five-foot-long double-edged and sharply pointed weapon. It can't be documented, but Caesar's legions were known never to have lost a battle when his broadswordsmen led the attack.

Caesar, again out of his own pocket, provided his legions with another proven ultimate weapon that again and again proved to be unstoppable by the enemy. It was an oversized, lightweight long spear about two feet longer than the standard spear that the enemy would have. The Roman soldiers would march up to the enemy spearmen and, with the extra length of their spears, hold them back from attacking, while Caesar's bowmen would stand behind the long-spearmen, and shoot thousands of arrows at the enemy without ever having to put themselves in danger from the enemy. If the Roman legions ever took to the field to fight a pitched battle, they rarely, if ever, would lose due to the overwhelming forces put into play.

All men in battle were required to have fifteen days of food on them at all times. This was always a problem for a marching army, and that was why Caesar went to Egypt (Cleopatra) to personally secure his needed supply of food for his legions.

Female camp followers and servants were always allowed to follow and service their masters and others who were putting in their years of service in the Legions. Caesar personally paid all expenses for the female camp-followers who moved around with the army.

It must be noted that the great Caesar also supported a

large naval fleet of warships. It was bigger, stronger and better trained than any other fleet in the civilized world at that time. After the tragic death of Julius Caesar, it was his nephew Augustus Caesar who used the always-ready and standing-by fleet of warships to defeat Mark Antony and Cleopatra.

When his officers had gathered for their morning briefing, Caesar had decided to send each of the six legions into the countryside surrounding Rome so that they could take up positions covering the three entry and exit sides of the huge city. He was not worried about the river's fourth side of the city, since the fleet was sitting there quietly on standby alert.

He dispatched each one of his six personal bodyguards to accompany each Legion to their appointed positions, and when the army was in place, each of the bodyguards would catch up with him at the Senate where he would wait for their confirmation that everyone was in place. Then he was going to announce his formal takeover of Rome as the new dictator for life.

With his legions controlling the key points into and out of the city, there would be no way that he could be opposed in his planned takeover. (This explains why six of his seven personal body-guards were not present when he was assassinated later on that day.)

After the tent had cleared of all the general staff members, Caesar picked up an apple from the few that were sitting on his desk, and stepped outside for his ride to the Senate, which was in central Rome. Caesar was thinking that after he finished securing his final appointment as Dictator of Rome, he would be ready to move out on his next campaign, which was still in the planning stage.

Even though he had come to an understanding with Cleopatra about the steady supply of food, he did not feel perfectly comfortable trusting her without any control over the supply situation. He would move out one of his six legions to the outskirts of her Egyptian city, and in that way keep the pressure on her to deliver on her promise to give him exclusive rights to her food supplies.

This would also give him a reason to take a few days off every so often to visit with the young Cleopatra. She was a beautiful young lady, and she seemed more than willing to be his eager and quite aggressive bed partner.

With these happy thoughts in mind, Caesar stepped into the now-waiting chariot and held onto the support rail as they took off at a fast pace. Caesar knew that this older-model chariot was a back-up, because his regular and more stylish one needed to have a broken wheel repaired. It was planned for his driver/bodyguard to go and pick it up after he dropped Caesar off at the Senate Building. There were several important people that Caesar had scheduled to visit in the late afternoon, and he wanted to arrive in his stylish chariot rather than in the back-up one. (We now know the answer as to why this body-guard would not be with Julius Caesar when he was attacked later on in the day.)

The ride through the bumpy streets of Rome was uneventful and fairly rapid. From the army camp outside the city limits to the Senate drop-off point took about an hour. Caesar got off, waved good-by to his driver, and walked up the many stairs that led to his reserved location at the top of the Senate seats.

Julius Caesar's mind was whirling with all the details of what he had to do after the voting on a few Senate bills that were coming up for discussion. He did not pay attention to the missing guards because they were always in the background and he hardly ever noticed them even when they were there watching everything. (This accounts for the lack of guards inside the Senate building at the time of the attack on Caesar.)

§

Caesar hated to admit it, but the climb to the top of the Senate seats was getting harder and harder. He had to stop twice before he finally arrived at his spot and was able to sit down. He always promised himself at these moments that he would work out with his troops and get himself back into proper physical condition. He had good intentions, but something always came up and needed his attention at that moment.

He was just sitting there quietly, waiting for the Senate to be called to order, when he noted several of the Senators climbing up toward him. They were probably going to ask him for his opinion on one of the bills that the Senate was going to be talking about this morning. He smiled to himself as he saw that one of the approaching Senators was his old enemy—or should he be calling him his new friend—Marcus Brutus.

Caesar had let Brutus stay alive after Caesar had defeated him in a little fight over something or other. Caesar could not remember exactly what it was that they had fought about with their personal soldiers. Brutus had sworn allegiance to Caesar, and allowed Caesar to buy him a Senate seat. He had promised to always vote for anything Caesar wanted him to in the Senate. From that day forth, Caesar always knew that he had one more Senator who would always vote for everything he told them to vote for. Caesar liked having an inside man in the rule-making Senate, and he especially enjoyed holding it over Brutus's head that he was a bought man. (So now we know why Caesar did not have his enemy, Brutus1killed when he had the opportunity to do so).

At that time, Caesar's logic was good, but for the long term, that decision was going to be bad for him as he watched Brutus and the other Senators make their way slowly up the steep stairs that led to where Caesar was sitting.

§

A bit of background information is important if we are to understand the who, what, when and where of the world-shaking event that was about to happen.

The Ides of March is the name of the fifteenth day of March in the early Roman calendar. That was the actual day, in the year 44 BCE, that Julius Caesar, self-proclaimed dictator of Rome, was assassinated inside the Roman Senate chambers.

There is a historical rumor that has been around for centuries that a fortune teller (called a soothsayer in those days) had said to Caesar, as he left for the Senate, that something terrible was going to happen to him if he left the security of the military camp where he was staying with the troops. The author personally believes the famous playwright, William Shakespeare, in one of his plays, made up those lines, and then gave the soothsayer credit for having said, "Great Caesar, beware the Ides of March!" Either way, it does not matter how the idea of the Ides of March got into the public awareness. It is there, and it stands for bad times. Since the time of Caesar's violent death, March fifteenth has forever been marked as a day of infamy, and it has fascinated scholars and writers of history ever since.

The assassination of Julius Caesar set off major changes within the city of Rome, and that in turn had a ripple effect throughout the known world. Rome controlled, by force of arms, three-quarters of the continent of Europe. When something this major happened to one of its leaders, the whole civilized world felt its effects.

Before Julius Caesar declared himself to be the dictator of Rome, the city had a republican form of government that was headed by two consuls, or heads of their respective political parties. It was Caesar's removing the old form of government that directly led to his being killed. In those days, if you disliked something a politician did to you or said about you, you had him killed in a violent way so as to make a statement to your enemies.

Julius Caesar made a huge personal mistake when he publicly turned down the offer of becoming the king of the Roman empire if he would be patient and wait for the slow-moving process to proceed. He was quoted as saying that it would take too long for it to happen, and so he declared himself dictator, which took effect immediately.

The strength behind Caesar's move to declare himself dictator for life was based on his large standing army that he had stationed on the edge of the city of Rome. His terrible error in judgement that led to his death, was when, for whatever reason, he did not take his personal bodyguards with him as he always did when he entered the grounds of the Senate, where his enemies were always around him.

Had Caesar taken proper precautions to protect himself, then his best and most personal friend, Mark Antony, would not have left Rome, since Julius Caesar would have still been alive. But Mark Antony did leave Rome after Caesar's death, and he did fall in love with the beautiful Cleopatra, and he did become her full-time lover and he did live with her in Egypt.

Mark Antony was later killed in a huge sea battle against Julius Caesar's nephew, who took over control of the Roman dictatorship. The nephew's name was Augustus Caesar. He had the month of August named after himself, and the reason he did so was because he could!

After the difficult defeat of Mark Antony, who used the Egyptian army as his own, Augustus Caesar had no more major enemies, and he declared himself dictator for life just as his uncle Julius had—only Augustus Caesar went about becoming dictator for life in a more efficient way.

He had all of his enemies in the senate killed or outlawed immediately, and then he declared himself dictator. There was no opposition left to oppose him, and he became the first of many Caesars to hold the lifetime office. Augustus, who was a bit wiser when it came to protecting himself than his uncle Julius was, always took bodyguards with him whenever he left the palace.

And finally you need to know that there were many other Caesars in the family line, but perhaps the most infamous of them all from those most interesting times was Nero Caesar, who was supposed to have fiddled while Rome was burning. History tells us that the story about Nero Caesar was just another made-up story about another much-hated dictator named Caesar.

§

HERE IS A BIT MORE HISTORICALLY ACCURATE INFORMATION ON THE JULIUS CAESAR STORY

Julius Caesar had really offended the common citizens of Rome in another very important way, which was religiously. Religion has always had a major role in our world's history, and Caesar's screw-up was another case of bad judgement.

All Rome's gold and silver coins for the entire empire had stamped on them the likenesses of gods and goddesses. When Caesar had his own face stamped on everyday coins, the public was greatly offended because they thought that he was telling everyone that he was greater than the gods themselves. The mistake here was that he lost the loyal public support that he used to have, and he had to depend only upon his standing army more and more.

The actual killers of Julius Caesar were elected officials from within the city called senators. It was the senators who voted on laws and day-to-day things that affected the daily lives of the citizens of the city. When Caesar declared that he wanted to be dictator for life, the senators knew that they would be removed from office, and they reacted by all agreeing to kill Caesar in a single group effort so that no one individual would stand out.

The only person that Caesar knew at all from among the senators was Marcus Brutus. The two of them had a history of sorts with each other and an uneasy truce existed between them. Marcus Brutus was a former general in the army who had lost a small battle to Julius Caesar over a problem that they could not settle by discussion. To settle their differences, they both brought their personal armies with them and fought a battle upon an open field just outside the Rome city limits. After much loss of life on both sides of the battlefield, the brilliant Caesar smashed Brutus's forces and was the victor of the battle. For reasons that we have already given, Caesar spared the life of Brutus.

Of course, Caesar had no way of knowing that within three years after having his life spared, the traitor Brutus would lead the senators on that day of the killing. The killing of Caesar happened as he took his regular seat, which was at the top of the senate chamber (where it was said by some unhappy senators that from there Caesar was always looking down on them).

One of the conspirators, with the others right behind him, came over to where Caesar was sitting and said loudly that he had a request to ask of Caesar.

Caesar, who was seated, turned to the senator as if to ask him what it was that he wanted to say, when the lead senator and all the others suddenly rushed up to Caesar and without hesitation began to stab him. A shocked Caesar tried to cover himself up by falling to the ground and roll himself up into a ball, but it was no use!!!

Before Caesar died, he recognized one of his attackers. It was the man he had granted his life back to. It was Marcus Brutus. It was later reported that Caesar cried out in fear and anger. *"Et tu, Brute?"* which, translated from the Latin, means, "You too, Brutus?"

The lesson from all of this, according to the playwright William Shakespeare, was to never forgive an enemy. Never give him a chance to come back at you. You must never forget someone who hates you, and you must destroy him before he destroys you! And then all will be well.

All of Caesar's killers ran off, but justice would catch up with them all later, and they were eventually all killed.

And finally, it was reported that as they carried the body

of Caesar through the streets of Rome, one of his hands was hanging down and dragging in the dirt.

§

Final facts on Julius Caesar:

Born Gaius Julian Caesar on July 13 of the year 100 BCE.

He died March 15 of the year AD 44. His age at death was 56.

Roman statesman, general and author. Famous for conquests of Gaul.

He changed the Roman republic into a Roman dictatorship and as a result changed the world.

BENJAMIN FRANKLIN
JANUARY 17, 1706–APRIL 17, 1790

Benjamin Franklin was one of the founding fathers of the United States of America. He was a renowned author, printer, political theorist, politician, postmaster, scientist, inventor, civil activist, statesman, and diplomat. And oh, how he loved the ladies!

What follows is a brief and entirely invented story, created by the author, as to how he met his future bride-to-be. The setting for this romantic incident is when he was a very young man, and fame and fortune were still many years ahead of him.

§

At the first whisper of sound, Benjamin was fully awake!

He had left his friend and host to his coffee, and excused himself by saying he was very tired and was going to try and get some sleep. The adventure that they had planned for the next day sounded very exciting, and it took him some time before he fell into a deep sleep.

And then the sound that awoke him happened! He became aware that the noise he heard was the soft *snick* of the well-oiled lock on the door leading into his room from the hallway. Someone had quickly cracked open the door and slipped into the room. Of this, Benjamin was certain!

Even though the door was again closed, and the room was in semi-darkness, he knew that someone was inside the room with him. His hand closed upon the hilt of the dagger he always kept under his pillow. Habits of a lifetime are hard to break.

Unable to clearly see, the room's intruder was probably waiting to orient himself within the complete darkness of the bedroom.

Ever so slowly, Benjamin slid from beneath his blankets and crept toward the almost indiscernible sound of soft breathing. As he stealthily closed upon his unseen visitor, Benjamin suddenly relaxed his tense grip upon his dagger. To his sensitive nostrils came the piquant fragrance of perfume. He swept out his arm and gathered in a startled female form.

The girl gave an involuntary yelp of surprise, then subsided in his embrace. A quick brush of his arm made it plain to him that the woman carried no weapon.

"I might have gutted you, young lady! It's a good thing that I heard your breathing and smelled your perfume. And wasn't that door locked? I do remember snapping the lock closed before I went to bed!"

"Anyone can pick locks. I have done it before. That doesn't matter, does it? The most important thing that counts is that I am here with you."

She was wearing only a thin shift. Benjamin, who was wearing rather less, was keenly aware of the warm female body that was pressed against his own bare flesh.

The girl was saying, "The master asked me to spend the night with you, and said that I was to be very good to you." As she was saying this, she pressed herself tightly against him.

Benjamin was thinking to himself that Michel really knew how to make a guest in his home feel very welcome. And now he was wondering if all the things he had heard about French girls were true or not. He realized that he was about to find out.

As he ran his hands over her in a brief caress, he determined that her shoulders were straight and almost mannish, her breasts were full and high, and her hips slender but generously curved. What more could one ask of so willing a female?

She rose on tiptoe to fully mold herself against his large

and powerful frame. Her mouth opened to receive the heated branding of his searching tongue. A soft moan escaped her lips as she felt a simmering heat in the very depths of her being.

Benjamin's ears were filled with the soft sounds coming from deep within her throat, as he held her crushed against him. His lips left her mouth, and he tasted the softness of her cheek, the fragile curve of her jaw, and the slim line of her throat. As he placed moist kisses along the upper edge of her shoulders, he felt the straining fullness of her breasts. He lowered his lips and placed feathery kisses between the valley created by her breasts, while his fingers brushed against hardened tips.

The girl inhaled sharply as she felt the soft caress of his fingers going down her spine. But she released her held breath just as quickly, as his head lowered once again down to her breasts. Sheer carnal desire flamed throughout her body as his lips settled over one rose-colored nipple. As he suckled the tender tip, her limbs weakened and she felt herself slipping to the floor.

Before she could fall very far, Benjamin gathered her up in his arms and stepped carefully into the small alcove that contained his large bed. Gently, he laid down upon the rumpled coverlet.

His mouth consumed her with its searching demand as his tongue pushed forward, and finding no resistance from the compliant female, he sought out each and every curve of her body as he once again traced a tempting path down to her ever-waiting breast. As he drew a sweet nipple into his mouth, her body trembled with a deep, wanton desire that left her clutching at his head and pressing herself fully against him.

It seemed only seconds later that she lay upon the coverlet with nothing covering her body. Her gown had been discarded upon the floor beside the bed, and for a breathless moment, Benjamin stared down at the wonderful curves of perfection that he could see in the darkened room. The heated flames within his eyes seared every inch of her flesh, as he gazed upon the fullness of her twin globes with their dusty rose-colored buds. His eyes roamed down the length of her trim rib cage to the tiny indent of her navel, and across the womanly flare of her hips, and down the long, shapely legs.

Benjamin at age twenty-six had bedded down a fair share of girls so far in his lifetime. Most of them were local girls from the British Colonies that were scattered over the eastern seaboard of America. There were also a few native Indian girls who came into and out of his life, and they were all very sexy and very exciting, as were the others.

But, he thought quickly, as he was really quite busy with the young lady who occupied his full attention at the moment, French girls were everything they said about them and more. Benjamin's gaze caressed the delicate ankles and slim feet of the beautiful French maid that his new friend Michel had sent to him. He knew that he now owed Michel a big favor, and one he would definitely make up in the future. But for the moment he was having one of the highlights of his young life!

He drew himself halfway up, eyes filling with burning desire as he looked down upon the junction of her womanhood, with the feathering of dark, curling hair lending a definite contrast to the creamy, pearly iridescence of her skin.

As his eyes returned to her face, she was parting her lips as if to speak, but seeing the desire in his eyes, she was content. At that moment, she knew that her master's guest desired her above anything else in his life. This indeed was raw female power and her own passion-laced desires welcomed his seduction. The irresistible pull of pleasure's promise grabbed her body as Benjamin's mouth again roamed over her.

With feathered kisses, licking and nibbling, he ravished her breasts once again. His straight white teeth caressed her flesh and driving her mad with her own desire. A soft moan escaped from her, deep within her throat and at the same time his dark head lowered to her ribs, and the tempting curves of her waist and hips.

The taste of her sweet flesh and the feel of her satin-smooth body combined to seduce Benjamin into a physical wanting that knew no bounds. His hands splayed over the firmness of her belly and then pressed on closer to her hips. His tongue sent flames shooting throughout the lower portion of her body, as he rubbed the inside of her thighs. As his mouth touched her woman's jewel, she bucked as sweet, forbidden pleasure snaked through her womb and thrashing limbs.

Without mercy, Benjamin kept up his love play, his tongue plunging into her moist, sweet depths, and lingering over the extremely sensitive nub as she shuddered again and again. Her cries filled his ears and fueled his desire to pleasure her to the fullest.

As the trembling of her body slowly subsided, and the fingers within his hair lessened their tight hold, Benjamin rose from his position between her thighs. His lips seared branding kisses over her body as he finally pressed his length of manhood against her. His eyes witnessed the sated passion on her face before he covered her mouth once more with his own.

The girl opened up to him, too swept up in the steaming rapture of the moment to do otherwise. As Benjamin's tongue filled her mouth, he felt the sculptured marble head of his love-tool pressing at the opening between her parted thighs.

His buttocks drew upward, and as he entered her, just an inch or so, he felt the tightness of her passage. Another thrust and another inch as he felt the velvet trembling of her inner sanctum. A low rumbling came from within his own chest and filled the entire room with his animal-like noises.

He moved back and forth, going slowly deeper and deeper and then with drawing back to the very lips of her moist opening. Over and over he plied her with his skillful seduction, until she was clutching his back with her head thrown back wildly as the fullness in her loins drove her toward a frenzy of mindless desire.

Each time the brand of his lance drove into her depths

and stirred her, her body moved toward completion. Her legs slowly rose and fell as she sought to capture and hold onto the entire length of him that was deep within her.

Still holding himself back somewhat, Benjamin caught hold of her buttocks, and with a talent born of past love-making, he maintained his inner control. Even as he felt the shuddering coming from the lady beneath him, he was able to inhale deep breaths of air, willing himself not to release the final fury of his passion.

Benjamin knew the power of her climax, and for a moment or two, he fought his own heated need that was racing through his own loins. He watched her passion-filled face and heard the climatic moans escaping from her throat. Each thrust was now torture-laced for him as he fought off the aching need for his own fulfillment.

Only when he felt her climax receding, did he allow himself to give full vent to his own desire. His mouth covered hers, and as he plunged just a fraction deeper into her soft velvety depths, wildfire absolutely caught within him. Scalding pleasure burst forth from the center of his being and showered upward, racing through his most powerful lance.

It took Benjamin several minutes to regain his normal breathing and to conquer the disbelief that filled his brain as he thought about the wonderful moment that had just occurred between himself and this woman. A slight shudder coursed .through him as he realized that he had never before been driven to such powerful feelings of lust and surely, he thought, she must have felt the same thing.

Turning his face so that he could gaze into her eyes, he found her eyelids closed, her breathing soft, and her arms caressing his neck. She slept peacefully in his arms, and a small smile filtered over his lips. It seemed quite silly, but he did not even know her name!

Tomorrow would be soon enough for all the adventures that Michel had promised him. For now, he just wanted to enjoy the moment. Sleep, slow and pleasant came to him in the most wonderful manner.

All was quiet within the darkened room.

WILLIAM BUTLER

THE FOLLOWING SHORT STORY IS FULL OF FAST
CARS, A BEAUTIFUL LADY, LOTS OF PASSION, AND A
STORY THAT IS SET IN TODAY'S MODERN WORLD.

The wind was just strong enough to make a feeble effort at
moving the leaves on the trees that lined the long driveway
in front of the restaurant. William had just given the parking
attendant a twenty-dollar tip as he took the keys from him,
while carefully helping Jackie into the passenger seat of his
newly purchased Mercedes.

While they were buckling up with the oversized seat belts,
Jackie had turned to him and asked him to tell her something
about this exceptional-looking car. She said that she knew that
it was one of a kind, and that she was sure that there was an
interesting history connected to it.

As he slowly pulled out of the restaurant's circular
driveway, William's mind was flashing back to last week when
he had been out looking for something new and different in a
high-end car.

He was in the showroom of the Mercedes dealership on
Wilshire Boulevard in Beverly Hills, when he saw three men
pushing something very black and very interesting onto the
showroom floor.

"What is that one coming in all about?" he asked the
salesman.

"Good question, sir! That is a specially made Mercedes model called an E-55. It is first cousin to the usual E4-30 that you are probably familiar with. This E-55 has been specially modified, and the exterior finish is something new in a special metallic black with parchment-leather upholstery."

"I can tell that it's something interesting! Tell me the story on this car. I just might be interested if it's really different and the price is right."

The salesman went over to a nearby desk, and after moving a few papers around, he pulled out a red folder. He went over to a copy machine that was in the far corner of the showroom and made two copies of the report. He then went back to the desk and returned the file into the drawer.

William was already sitting in the E-55's driver's seat, and the sales man opened up the passenger door and sat down with a pleased expression on his face. William assumed that James, the salesman, enjoyed talking about something different from the ordinary cars that passed through the showroom. And it was not every day that he could sit down and discuss something as interesting as the E-55.

William followed him with his eyes on his copy of the paperwork as James read out loud.

"This car is one of a kind, and it is very much out of the ordinary. It has a five-and-a-half liter V-9 engine that is more powerful than any other Mercedes that has ever been built! It has been brought up to three hundred fifty-four horse power, with a specially built transmission to make sure that it can basically handle all that power. The body itself has been lowered, and the suspension system has upgraded shock absorbers, anti-roll bars and two sets of very special springs. It has eighteen-inch wheels, special-rated oversized tires, and extremely heavy duty brakes."

William, who was listening carefully to every word that

was being said, was having trouble holding back his emotions and he told himself to calm down. James was still talking.

"The windows are tinted darkly enough to make the various occupants within the car unrecognizable, and after it arrived in the United States, we sent it out to a specialist to be lightly armored."

"What exactly do you mean when you say 'lightly armored'?" William asked.

James opened up his passenger-side door, pressed a button and the window rolled down halfway. "As you can easily see, the side glass is a lot thicker than the standard window glass. It is a full one-half inch thick, which is unheard of. And the roof, all the door panels and the floor pan have all been reinforced with extremely light-weight but very tough materials like Kelvar. The car will repel small-weapons fire, even heavy machine-gun fire, but it won't, of course, be able to stop a bazooka or a land-mine. You would need the fully armored version for that level of protection."

The salesman went on. "You have sport seats and special trim all the way around, and there is also a specially concealed radar scrambler under the dashboard," he said as he looked around to see if anyone else was listening to their conversation.

"I love the car! What's your asking price?"

"Actually, this car doesn't belong to this agency," the salesman replied in a quiet voice. "It's the property of the widow of a former client of ours, a South American gentleman."

"And why is she a widow?" Michael asked with a big smile on his handsome face.

"The car was delivered a few days too late to serve the purpose for which the South American gentleman intended."

"You mean he was in another car when ..."

"When he needed the extra protection that this car would have afforded him."

"And tell me, James, how much does the sad widow want for the car?"

"Something in the neighborhood of $_____."

He named a figure and William touched his inside jacket pocket to make sure that he had his checkbook with him.

"Ask the widow if she will accept my offer of $_____." William named a number. "And please tell her that it will be my one and only offer."

"Let me make a telephone call," the salesman said. He went to his desk and picked up the telephone.

§

William snapped back to reality and remembered that the beautiful Jackie had just asked him a question about the car.

"To answer your question, Jackie, I must confess that I don't know too much about the original owner. I was told that he had recently passed away, and the family had no use for such a big car. I happened to be at the right place at the right time, and now this baby belongs to me! I'm glad you like it."

While they were talking, William was driving down Wilshire Boulevard, which took them from Beverly Hills into the Westwood area of Los Angeles. This area was built around the UCLA campus. William had purchased an apartment in one of the many high-rise buildings that were everywhere in the West Los Angeles/Westwood area.

The Mercedes was given to the doorman as William led the way into the elevator which took them up to the twenty-fifth floor.

There was no hesitation on Jackie's part going with him to his apartment. She was very attracted to William, and if it led to sleeping with him on the first date, she really didn't care.

Her ideas was to simply do things so well, that she would overshadow the other women she knew he'd had in his bachelor lifestyle. It wasn't often that she met such a successful, good-looking and well-educated guy, and she was going for the brass ring, no matter what.

It was drilled into her head that good girls did not sleep with their dates until at least the third date, but wasn't this really the second time they were together? The first one being at the restaurant where they first met last week.

The hell with it, she thought. She was prepared to go all the way if she had to! The worst that she could do was have the great sex that she knew was in front of her. Where was the downside. and just what did she have to lose?

And so, with a light spirit and a good attitude, she stepped into his apartment on the twenty-fifth floor that looked down upon the entire world. The door was unlocked and she stepped into the entry way and was immediately enchanted.

Jackie stepped into a large entry way that led them into a huge room off to the left of the foyer entrance. It was a study or an office of some sort. There was a beautiful and quite massive desk that seemed to be carved out of one single piece of unstained wood. It just dominated the room with its aged handles and trim that went around the entire desk. A multi-colored greenish blotter lay precisely centered on the desk with a set of four differently colored marking pens lying there in a neat row.

The walls were surrounded with rich wooden shelves which groaned with the weight of books, drums, masks and old weaponry that looked like they all came from very exotic lands. Jackie was immediately attracted by a wall space between the shelves, which was occupied by brightly colored shields that were fronted by two crossed swords. One set was an ancient English kite shield holding another two crossed swords, and the other was an African Zulu buffalo-hide shield with scimitars. Jackie knew that museums would jump at the chance, if they could only get their hands on a collection half this rich and so interestingly varied.

William led her further into the apartment, showing her

the wealthy splendor of hardwood floors and custom-carved wood statues and fountains and several real-looking suits of armor.

They spent over an hour looking at several original paintings that added a great deal of class and bright colors to the walls. One of the ones she knew was an original Van Gogh. Most impressive!

Despite trying not to be, Jackie realized that she was curious beyond words, as to just who and what William really was. She realized that he had to be more than just an Assistant History Professor at UCLA, which he said he was. He had to be much more than that just to justify all the things she saw and all the things she was slowly finding out about him. She confirmed her earlier resolve to herself, that no matter what was required of her this evening, she was going to be okay with it.

They ended up standing with drinks in hand in front of the dining room's clear glass window that looked down on the Westwood campus of the University. The city lights were overwhelming from this point of view. The two of them seemed content and happy to be with each other as they continued to stand there holding hands and just looking out into the distance.

It wasn't long until William's fingers slid carefully around her soft neck, as he tenderly kissed her with a very slow, sexy lingering kiss.

Jackie sighed deeply and returned his kiss, as she wrapped her arms around this great hunk of masculinity. She felt herself unable to resist the sweet, hot warmth of his tongue against hers. The feel of his hands running over her back as he held her close seemed so right. It felt good to have him touch her as she felt the heat of his body coming through to her.

Suddenly, they were deeply kissing each other, drinking in a deep intensity that seemed so very special.

Jackie felt like she would simply die if she did not have more of him. Her tongue stroked his in return.

He twined his fingers into her hair, tugging away the band

holding it at the nape of her neck. He continued to angle her mouth to his, taking more of her, and it was still not enough for him.

She leaned firmly into him and felt the thick ridge of his erection melding to her moving hips.

"You feel good," he murmured, "so damn good!"

William wrapped his arms around her and pulled her closer, twining his fingers in her silky hair. He inhaled the familiar scent of roses that was so much this woman. It was a wonderful sensation.

With his mouth held gently over hers, his tongue continued to caress her, in long, languid strokes that had them both moaning with the contact, with the connection, with the sudden burning between them. Seconds ticked by and they were still satisfied just kissing, softly and tenderly.

William hardly remembered how his shirt, pants and shoes came off, but he remembered everything about undressing Jackie. He roughly pulled her top upward and over her head, and quickly unhooked her nicely overflowing bra, and unzipped her skirt.

Jackie tossed her clothing aside as William quickly filled his hands with her high, full breasts and stroked her plump pink nipples. He gently pressed her back against the nearest wall, his gaze devouring her almost naked body, while she helped remove whatever jewelry she still had on. She left on her dark stockings, garter belt and panties. She kicked aside her accumulated clothing as he went down to his knees in front of her.

His hands quickly went to her hips and his lips slid down to her flat stomach. "Finally," he breathed out. "I have been looking forward to this all evening!" He slid his hands delicately to her backside, while he bent his head, brushing his lips over her hips, trailing kisses over to her midsection, widening the space between her thighs and kissing her very slowly. He explored the intimate vee of her body, his fingers teasing the slick wet heat of her sexual arousal that he felt coming on.

He suddenly stood up and scooped her off of her feet, as easily as if she were a mere child, and headed to the far end of the apartment toward his bedroom.

Moonlight was spilling into the large master bedroom as William carefully deposited Jackie on her back in the center of the huge bed. He thoughtfully placed an oversized pillow beneath her head to ensure her comfort.

William pressed his lips to hers, slid his tongue carefully into her mouth once again as the sweetness of her completely filled his senses. He tasted her with his eyes, seeking the flavor of her open- ness, her willing-ness and possibly the beginning of her love.

His eager hands roamed freely over her willing body, and she shivered with pleasant chills running up and down her spine. He palmed her breasts once again, teasing her nipples and plucking them into tight little peaks.

Jackie gently wrapped her hand around the base of his erection, and William could actually feel himself thicken with her touch and the anticipation of what was yet to come. She guided him to the wet slick center of her body, and she felt him shaking with his urgent need. He seemed to be trying to resist pushing into her on his own, rather than waiting for her to take him there. She easily pressed his throbbing shaft inside her, as she slid down the length of him, taking him in all at once.

William was thinking about how hot and tight she was, and how she was so wet for him, and she felt ever so good! Raw hunger rose inside him as he moaned loudly while pressing her down deeply into the softness of the bed, and lifted her hips to allow him to smoothly thrust inside of her.

Her body tightened around his throbbing erection as she took him hard and deep inside of her. Her fingers were in his hair, and their soft touches sent shivers up and down his spine.

He just loved her kisses, those delicate, sweet kisses that could be so wild and wicked and yet at the same time, so soft and feminine! Jackie seemed to be everything that he wanted her to be. Could she be the one that he was searching for all these years?

He was still hungry for her as she seemed to be for him. It was in their every move, in their every touch, in their every groan of great pleasure. If they could have melted into each other and become one, they would have done just that at that moment.

Jackie leaned back as William's hands settled on her flat stomach, pumping himself into her, as she allowed him to ride her in their erotic dance. Her beautiful breasts swayed with the rhythm of their bodies and her nipples seemed to be calling for his mouth once again. She spiked her fingers again through his hair with her moans turning into sexy little pants of pleasure that were driving her wild.

William knew that he was coming to the end of his ability to hold back from the final bursting of his manhood into her welcoming body, and he pushed and thrust with the final moments of the glorious pleasure that she was giving him.

"Yes, William," she moaned, burying her face in his neck. "So … good … William …"

With his name on her lips, asking him to pleasure her for the last time, he was driven over the edge. He could not hold himself back any longer.

For the two of them, almost in perfect timing, the room disappeared, and the present moment also disappeared, because there was only the flush of completion to the wonderful sex act that they shared. As they both came to final completion, the two of them just collapsed into each other's arms and laid there, unable to move. For long seconds, they clung to one another, skin damp and breathing heavily.

"I love you, William! I really do! I never felt something like this before!"

And with her words bouncing around inside his head, he held her close and softly kissed her lips as they both fell into a deep and most pleasant sleep.

WILLIAM BUTLER TIME TRAVELER

I HOPE YOU ENJOYED MEETING UP WITH WILLIAM, WHO IS ONE OF MY NEWEST AND MOST UP TO DATE HEROS.

WILLIAM, NOT ONLY DRIVES THE HOTTEST CAR IN TOWN, BUT HE IS ALSO INTO SWORD FIGHTING.

HOW DO THE TWO MIX IN WITH HIS LOVE AFFAIRS? READ ON …

"EN GARDE, WILLIAM"

THE TIME FRAME FOR THIS SPECIAL LITTLE ADVENTURE IS CURRENT AND THE YEAR IS NOW

§

William turned quickly and looked behind him. He had just heard someone call out his name.

She stood a dozen paces from him, a tall slender girl with dark eyes and close-cropped brown hair. She wore a fencing jacket and held a rapier/sword in her right hand. In her left, she held a protective fencing mask.

She was looking directly at William and laughing at the same time. Her teeth were white, even and a trifle long, and a band of freckles crossed her small nose and the upper portions of her well-tanned cheeks.

There was that special air of vitality about her, which is

attractive in many ways quite different from mere comeliness. This was especially true when viewed from William's vantage point of having known so many women.

She saluted him with her blade. *"En garde, William!"* she said.

§

My name is William Butler, and I do answer to being called Will, Bill or William, but at that particular moment, I was tired and was not in the mood for any games.

I had just come off of a full two-hour session of fencing with my fencing instructor on the mats, where we were going at it hot and heavy against each other. Today was my final session with him, and after eighteen long months of training and conditioning, I had finally advanced to the level where I could take him to a draw.

This was a real accomplishment, and I was very proud of having accomplished so much is such a little amount of time. My instructor was the equivalent of a black belt in the fine art of fencing, and for me to duel with him and come out even gave me the same top rating he had. I was very pleased with myself.

I knew that I was pretty good, and that I should be able to hold my own with anyone in a fencing situation. At least I hoped so, because I soon would be putting my life on the line, and only my skill with a sword would keep me alive.

Just a few minutes ago, I had received hugs and well-wishes from all my fencing friends at the studio when I had said my final farewells to them.

I had just walked outside and went over to the nearby baseball field, where I was just standing quietly, drinking a soft drink, when the girl with the mask and fencing equipment suddenly appeared.

"Who the hell are you?" I asked as I noticed another fencing jacket, a mask and a sword lying at her feet. Obviously, she had something in mind!

"No questions and no answers," she said. "At least not until we've fenced. I want to see for myself if you are as good as everyone says you are. You're not afraid of a mere girl, are you?"

I walked over and picked up the equipment. I could see that it would be easier to fence rather than argue with her. The fact that she knew my name disturbed me, and the more that I thought about it, the more she seemed somehow familiar.

It was best to humor her, I decided, as I shrugged into the jacket and buckled it on. I picked up the blade, tested it with a few simple moves and satisfied, I then pulled on the mask.

"All right," I said, sketching out a brief fencing salute to her, and then I advanced slowly toward her.

She moved forward also, and we met somewhere near first base on the flat baseball field.

I didn't bother to tell her that I was nearly exhausted from my dueling with my instructor for the past few hours. I just had to consider this to be an extra endurance training session.

She came at me very fast with a bare-feint-feint-thrust!

My riposte was twice as fast as her first move but she was good and was able to parry it and came back at me with equal speed. This was proving to be a good match, and I began to enjoy myself.

I began a slow backward retreat, trying to draw her out and expose a weakness, but she showed me nothing and laughed at me, and then came back, pressing me hard!

She was really well trained, and very athletic in all her quick responses. She obviously knew how good she was, and she wanted to show off what she could do, and I knew that I had to be ready for anything she would throw at me.

I was familiar with most of her classic attacks, but it was when she would improvise, that I had the most problems. She almost got through my defenses twice, in a low line attack, and I chalked up that move to something that I had never seen before, but would surely be ready for if I ever saw it again. She was teaching me things by actual live combat that my instructor never was able to give me. I was most impressed with my opponent at this moment.

I caught her with a beautifully executed double-stop-thrust as soon as she slowed down her offensive move. She had to fall back sharply, and I heard her curse softly, but good-naturedly, as she definitely acknowledged my excellent counter move.

I was really proud of the way my body responded automatically to the ebb and flow of our engagement. I felt that I really was at the top of my game, and I was suddenly loving this pickup duel being fought on a baseball field in the middle of the west side of Los Angeles.

I do not ordinarily like to fence with women, no matter how good they are, but this time, I discovered that I was actually enjoying myself. The skill and grace with which she carried the attacks and bore them at me gave me pleasure to behold and respond to.

I found myself thinking; what kind of mind did she have behind that mask? At first, I had wanted to tire her out quickly in order to conclude the match and put some questions to her. Now that we were really getting into it, I found myself wanting to prolong this highly enjoyable encounter. I was pleased that she did not tire readily!

I completely lost track of time as we stamped back and forth along the baseball path with our blades clicking steadily. A long while must have passed, though, before she finally stamped her heel to the ground as a signal, and then threw up her blade in a final salute to me.

She tore off her mask and gave me a great big smile. "Thank you," she said, breathing heavily.

I returned her salute, and drew off my own mask. I turned and fumbled with the jacket buckles, and before I realized it, she had approached and kissed me on the cheek.

I felt momentarily confused but I managed to smile at her. Before I could say anything, she took my arm and turned me back in the direction from which I had just come.

"You are wonderful," she said! "I think you deserve a reward! What do you say to a "quickie" at my place? It isn't far."

THE DUELING DAMSEL

Her name was Barbara Bennett, and she was a former United States fencing team member.

She would do workouts at the same place where I was upgrading my skills with swords and other weapons of the seventeenth century.

(Author's note: in case you are wondering about my reference to weapons of the seventeenth century, all things will be cleared up and concluded in the short story following this one.

William Butler, owner of a fantastic automobile and a home in Westwood, California, that is the envy of all who see it, a duelist of considerable skill, is also a time traveler whose final adventure will be opened and closed in the next story.)

And now to continue our story.

§

Now, I was beginning to remember why she had looked so familiar to me.

Whenever my instructor and I would do one of our special weapons workouts, a small group of students and teachers would gather around us to observe. I remembered her now, as the tall, cute one who had that great looking body, and who was always looking at me from a distance. Well, she was no longer any distance away now!

121

We had walked over to Westwood Boulevard at Wilshire, which was about three long blocks away from the baseball field, and then we walked up the two flights of stairs that led to her neatly appointed apartment.

We had talked as we walked, and I found out that she was an assistant manager at a local McDonalds restaurant where she worked four days a week.

Today was one of her days off, and she had gone to the dueling academy for a workout this morning, where she saw the final match that I had with my instructor.

The rest is history in that here I was in her apartment, waiting for her to come out of the bathroom where she had excused herself and gone to wash up after I finished with my own cleanup.

Her only instructions to me were to please close the curtains, and to leave some of the lights on in the bedroom. She also added, as she closed the bathroom door behind her, "Would you please pull back the covers on the bed and kindly strip down to your shorts."

This rather surprised me in that I had never met any female as aggressive as Barbara was. She really liked to be in charge, and with my being a guest in her home, I was okay with that.

I did all the household chores that she had asked of me, and I did strip down as I sat on the edge of the bed waiting for her to make an appearance. I was quite curious as to what I would be seeing when she came out of the bathroom. Would I be seeing a naked Barbara, or a sexy-outfitted lady, or perhaps even something else!

As it turned out, it was to be the something else, and I was pleasantly surprised by this girl who liked to be different!

Barbara had stepped into the bathroom and washed up. She shed all her clothing and looked carefully at her naked figure in the full-length bathroom mirror.

She really liked what she was looking at, and went about

getting dressed in the new "kinky" outfit that had looked like fun when she picked it out at the sexy lingerie boutique on Westwood Boulevard.

She stepped into what seemed to be the leg portion of a black thong, and worked it up and over her hips. She stared down at it, trying to figure out how to put on the top. She finally realized that the bra portion consisted of several individual straps that surrounded her breasts in a triangle shape with little chains draping down over each breast.

She pulled it on, exhilarated by the feel of the cold silver chains brushing against her nipples. There were five chains over each breast, and ... oh ... each center chain had a separated metal ring in the middle and that one sat right over her nipple. As she adjusted the leather straps on the bra so that they sat just right, her nipples blossomed, sticking forward through the rings.

She then opened the shoe box to find a pair of black leather shoes, with four-inch spike heels and wide ankle straps with matching silver studs. She pulled the shoes on and fastened all the straps.

She forced herself to peek at her image in the bathroom's full-length mirror. Her eyes widened with excitement. She looked ... erotic ... wicked ... and wildly sexy!

She noted another chain draped over the crotch area of her new leather outfit. She flicked it with her finger and realized that there was a slit in the fabric beneath it, running through the entire length of the crotch.

It was this opening that she hoped would allow William to find her special area, and she was hoping that he would know all kinds of ways to make use of it.

A final touch of perfume sprayed here and there, and then she was ready to open the door.

William jumped to his feet when the door opened, and he riveted his gaze upon her.

Barbara was just loving the amazed look on his face as she

walked over to him and kissed him on the lips with a light, feathery touch. Then she pushed him a few feet backward until he was sitting up on the edge of the bed watching her with his curious eyes.

Knowing that he was completely focused on her butt, she slowly turned and walked away from him over to the music comer, where she pressed the right buttons and her favorite slow-sounding rhythm filled the room.

In her younger days, Barbara had worked in a local and very high-end bar where she was one of the highly-featured pole dancers. She had worked out a very sexy series of moves that she began to perform in front of William, who was just sitting there, perfectly still, with his mouth hanging open in complete surprise. Obviously, he didn't know what to expect.

When she had mentioned the word "quickie" to him after their duel, he probably expected to jump into her bed, do his thing, and then get out in no time at all. That was not the way she liked having a sexual encounter!

Only when she was fencing did she do things quickly and precisely. When it came to sex, the slower and more original it could be, the better it always was for her.

There she was, swaying back and forth in front of William, when suddenly he could not sit still any longer. He had to touch her, caress her, and make passionate love to her. He stood up and put his arms completely around her, and held her close as he gently put his lips on hers in a soft and very sensual kiss.

Her response was also surprisingly gentle, and she carefully forced her darting tongue to move between his lips where it met no resistance.

They clung to each other for a few minutes until his hands began to roam down her shapely back.

The music in the background simply faded away, as he gently grabbed her buttocks and pulled her tightly against him.

She pulled her lips away from his so that she could take a moment and catch her breath. She liked the feel of his hands on her butt, and she snuggled up tighter against his hard body.

Still standing, he suddenly spun her completely around until she was standing directly in front of him.

She could feel the hardness of his erection pressed up against her back side. She noted that somehow or other, he had lost the pair of shorts that he had been wearing a few minutes ago, and this excited her even more.

A sudden jolt of electricity flashed through her body, as both of his hands went around her. His hands moved up to her breasts, where he began a gentle rubbing against her nipples, still protruding at full attention through the circular openings in the black bra that she was still wearing.

One of his hands slid down and moved about on her flat belly, and it was simply wonderful having her stomach rubbed at the very same time as one of her nipples was being gently pulled.

In a very practiced move, he grabbed hold of the top leather bra with all the little silver chains rattling about, and flipped it over her head. She was still standing in front of him facing away, as both of his hands began roaming all over her now free-standing breasts.

As she stood there enjoying the playtime that William was having with her "boobs," a random thought came to her. Can a guy tell by his sense of touch if a girl has had a boob job? Can William tell that what used to be an athletic, flat-chested girl was now a very well-endowed bra size 34 B-cupped female?

When she had the surgery a few years before, she had thought about making her breasts even bigger but decided not to do so for two very good reasons. The first one was that, as the famous old saying goes, "more than a handful is wasted," and secondly, they would get in the way whenever she was playing at being a sword-fighter.

What pleased her the most, after spending many sleepless nights thinking about it, was that she seemed to not have lost any of the sensations that touching her breasts gave her after the gel implants were put in. It was really hard to tell, but she thought that maybe the sensations were greater now, because after her surgery, she felt that much more sexy than she ever did before.

She greatly enjoyed watching the guys who never gave her a look before suddenly paying attention to her every move. A man's weakness is definitely a woman's tits! She loved simply ignoring those guys who didn't know she was alive when she was flat-chested. *Screw them*, she would think. *I'm in command now!*

With her slim and athletic body, and a set of good-sized knockers, she had her pick of the male population for many miles around. Her pick today was the famous William Butler.

She had watched him earlier this afternoon, and she saw firsthand, that he was extremely good with a pointed blade in his skilled hand. The question that she wanted to find out the answer to now was if he was any good with his personal blade!

SEX AND THE POLE DANCER

Pure, raw lust tore through William's system as he held Barbara close. He knew that she enjoyed wearing those black leather shorts and the high-heeled shoes, but they had to go. They would just be in his way! With little effort at all, he guided her into the removal of the shorts and shoes, and she stood before him, as naked as he was, and she knew that this was a good thing.

Barbara was swamped with many different sensations as she assisted William in the removal of her shorts and shoes. She thought that the sexy clothing was a good idea, and they were fun for a few minutes, but obviously he did not want them on her, and so she abandoned them without a second thought. She had absolutely no problem shedding them as she once again put her arms around his neck and pressed herself up against him. His lean and rock-hard body felt good to her!

He was holding her against himself effortlessly, with her feet off the ground, and she was just dangling there as he held her with his strong masculine arms. She felt his heavy erection pressing against her thigh and this was greatly exciting to her. He was big, and she knew that she was going to love every moment of the wonderful sex with him that was only moments away.

William stared down at her, seeing that her pale blue eyes were lit with a great hunger, which only he could satisfy right now. Hell, he thought to himself. This was one really hot woman!

He had come across this particular kind of female before, and he knew that it would take a lot of different climaxes and positions before she would be sexually satisfied. He was confident that he knew just what had to be done and he felt that he had the proper training for the job. Outside of his history books, which were his first love, being able to pleasure a woman was one of his main goals in life.

He had put in a lot of field work on learning just what went where and why, and he felt he was at the top of the leader board when it came to women. He was fully aware that he did not understand the female mind, and he knew that he had no clue as to how to decipher their emotions, but when it came to fooling around with sex, he was the perfect guy.

Enough with the thinking and more with the doing! This little lady was red-hot and ready to go!

He held her close and spun them both around in a circle just to celebrate their nakedness, and to get them ready for the fun that was in store for the two of them. He loved the way her hands clenched his shoulders and her nails as they lightly dug into his flesh. He laid her down gently on her back on top of the soft and giving bed, and then he leaned over her as her fingers speared into his curly hair as she pulled him toward her eagerly awaiting mouth.

She was loving it as much as he was! She loved his lips

on her lips, so hungry and deep as they continued to exchange more passionate kisses that sent flames rushing through all of her pulsating parts.

He gently moved himself between her moving thighs and found no resistance at all from her. She seemed hot and ready. He heard her whisper softly into his ear, "Make me feel you, William! Give me everything you've got! I can handle it!"

Without another word, William entered her place of pleasure and penetrated her very slowly, going back and forth and in and out. He would go a little farther with each push until he was finally in as far as he could go. Her sounds of pleasure began to multiply as he slowly increased the pace, and he pounded away at her very yielding and demanding body.

William, who always prided himself at being a breast man, had hold of one of her boobs as he continued to service her. In life, at least in William's young life, there was nothing like entering a woman, pounding away at her, and at the same time playing with her boobs. Sometimes, he thought, life was good, and this was one of those special moments!

After a few more minutes of these delightful sensations, William took advantage of his being very strong and Barbara being so slender and lightweight. While he was still inside her, he held her tightly and rolled himself onto his own back, which put her up on top of him in an upright sitting position.

She was actually sitting on his lap and now she could control their movements as she went up and down on him with a great smile on her pretty face. It was quite obvious to him that she had been on top of guys before, because she went at it with a recklessness and several moments later she rocked for the final time and moved herself backward, which caused him to completely slip out of her vagina. The two of them collapsed and neither of them moved for several long and wonderful minutes as they each fought to catch their breath.

William would have been content to just lie there and relive the moments, but not so Barbara. She began to fondle and kiss his shrunken penis, and under her well-educated hands, he began to grow hard once again. She was a miracle worker!

William was thinking that Barbara was the most sexual woman he had ever gone to bed with, and if he survived these experiences with her, he planned on courting her in a proper way and try and make her into a steady girlfriend. Not only was she cute with a great personality and figure, but she was one hot babe! William knew that someone like Barbara Bennett was rare, and he wanted to keep her in his life. He was no fool.

William knew that he was running out of gas, and that he had enough left for one final effort. Without speaking a word to her, he again lifted her up and put her face down on the bed. He put pressure on her shoulders so that she had to lean down on her arms in order to keep her balance. He put his arms around her waist and pulled her rear end up until she was on her knees.

He slipped himself carefully between her open legs, being careful not to hurt her, since she was probably sore and tender from all the friction the area was getting from him. Since she was so moist from all the other fooling around that they had been doing, he was able to slip his full length inside her quite easily.

Now in this position, the woman is actually quite helpless! All she can do is use her hands to keep her balance while she is being held face-down on the mattress. It is the man who is now in full control—and William took full advantage of the situation by pounding away as hard and long as he could.

He was only able to last a minute or so, and from the noises coming from Barbara who was now below him, he knew she was enjoying his male dominance over her. Moments later, they both collapsed into each other's arms, pulled the covers over themselves, and promptly fell into a deep and highly satisfied sleep.

NAPOLEON BONAPARTE

AND NOW, DEAR READER OF MINE, WE ARE COMING CLOSER TO OUR FINAL PHYSICAL AND SEXUAL ADVENTURES OF WHICH I AGAIN BRING IN WILLIAM AS OUR PROTAGONIST (THE HERO, OR GOOD GUY).

I AM GOING TO CLOSE THIS FINAL ROMP INTO ONE LAST HISTORICALLY ACCURATE AND SEXUALLY CHARGED ADVENTURE(S) OF WILLIAM, WHO IS OUR TIME-TRAVELER.

THE STORY OF WILLIAM IS IN MY PLANS FOR MY NEXT NOVEL, WHERE I WILL INCLUDE SOME OF THE ADVENTURES WE HAVE AREADY SHARED WITH HIM PLUS MANY MORE AS I TAKE HIM UPON AN EXQUISITE JOURNEY, VISITING AND DALLYING WITH THE MOST BEAUTIFUL AND MOST INTERESTING WOMAN THAT REAL-LIFE HISTORY HAS GIVEN TO US.

THANKS FOR THE READ AND FOR COMING ALONG FOR THE RIDE!!!

—BUD SELIGSON

AND AWAY WE GO

Paris was very different from the way it was three years ago when William and a current girl friend named Margo had run from landmark to landmark in streets and sidewalks that were spotlessly neat and clean.

That was in the year 2018, of course. The people of France

in the twenty-first century had come a long way from the dirty and dingy look that Paris had in the year 1776, where William was now.

1776 marked the fifth year that Queen Marie Antoinette ruled with her husband over all of the great country of France. She had been married to King Louis XVI at the age of fifteen, and being a spoiled teenager, things were just too easy for her.

Marie Antoinette continued to rule with her husband Louis until she was beheaded by the people of France in 1793 during the uprising that led to the French Revolution, which overthrew the monarchy. When she died at age 38, she was the most famous and most beautiful person to lose her life to the uprising.

Marie had a "small" palace of her own, along with several estates in the outskirts of Paris. And having just come out of her teenage years, she was still experimenting with her own personal sexual awakenings and awareness.

The people in the streets of Paris were talking about how bad the behavior of the royal couple was, and how they simply threw their riches around, while the poor people of the country were always watching and waiting for their chance to overthrow the government and the status quo.

William, who had been recently transported from the twenty-first century, could be seen on his first day in the Paris of 1776 stepping out of the small room that he had at the rear of a local church's grounds, and right into the proper timeline where Marie Antoinette was still the Queen of France.

(How he was transported into this important historical time is an issue that won't be dealt with at this time. A separate novel that will be following shortly will explain how this was done, so that we do not need to look at the how and why of time travel for now. For our storyline, here, we just have to accept the fact that he did time-travel, and that he did end up in Paris at the time of Marie Antoinette's rule.)

§

William had the key to a room at the rear of the church, and he carefully secured and locked it up.

He had brought several changes of clothing with him, so that on days that he planned to just walk the streets getting familiar with Old Paris, he would wear clothing that looked worn and not very fancy. His plan was to just fit in. In this way, he could go almost anywhere he wanted, and be just another face in the crowd, and that always worked very well for him.

He left his finest outfit hanging in the small closet for when he would crash the gate at the Queen's horse races and make his big play for her at the same time.

He carried with him at all times his sword, which was called a rapier in those days. He carried it on his left side in a secured scabbard that was tied to his belt. He could easily reach across his body and draw the sword with his right hand.

He also felt comfortable carrying a long, specially made twelve-inch double-sided dueling knife that had a needle-sharp point at the end.

His co-worker Josh from the university back home had traveled to Arkansas and gone to the factory that still was making the "Jim Bowie" style of knife that he wanted. William had placed an order for a very special knife with a very different set of specifications. William had insisted upon a knife that was two inches longer than a normal dueling knife and had both double-edged blades reinforced with a special steel alloy, in order to assure himself that the blade would not snap if he used it against other blades of these early Parisian streets.

The grip on the handle was also made to specially fit the exact contour and shape of William's right hand, and there was an added strap that went around his wrist in case he had to let go of the knife. This special strap looked like the leather that was in use in early Paris, but it was lined with a steel alloy that could not be cut by another blade if ever William found himself in a life-and-death dueling situation. He had spent an extra six months training in the specific science of close-up and very personal hand to hand knife fighting, and he felt confident that he could hold up very well if that kind of situation ever came up.

At that moment, he was standing where one day the world-famous shopping area of central Paris would be. Of course, he was thinking of the Avenue des Champs-Elysées, where for the right price the best clothing in the world could be purchased.

Normally he would be able to see several world-famous landmarks from where he was standing. From anywhere in Paris, the Eiffel Tower would be visible. It always amazed and fascinated him, that he could actually go anywhere he wanted and visit with anyone he wanted in their own personal time line. All of that could be done at the university, following the Time-Jump/Einstein Theory of transferring body mass from one overlapping time line to the next.

He had it in mind to write another book after he was all done with the Professor's project, and go back and visit some of history's greatest people like Julius Caesar, George Washington, President Lincoln, and perhaps some of the early Hollywood movie stars. Seeing a living Marilyn Monroe or an Elizabeth Taylor in all her glory would be one of the greatest adventures he could think of.

Also on his bucket list of things to do when he finished up the current project was to observe a Civil War battle and possibly watch former President Theodore Roosevelt as he led his men in a charge up the San Juan Hill during the Spanish-American War. Places to visit in history were like so many of the women he had taken to bed so far in his young life! By that, he meant that there were so many places (and women), and so little time.

Putting all thoughts of the future aside, he concluded his little walk at the empty lot where Mr. Eiffel was going to build his famous tower. Turning his attention to the south of where he was now standing at the future site of the Eiffel Tower, he saw the area where another famous Frenchman, Napoleon Bonaparte, would build his famous Arc de Triomphe (Arch of Triumph).

Napoleon had the Arch of Triumph built after he defeated the combined armies of several European countries, so that he could personally glorify his victory over the enemies of France.

William's mind was whirling for a moment as he reviewed in his mind the famous poem "The Charge of the Light Brigade" by Alfred, Lord Tennyson, a newspaper reporter who was an eyewitness to the last battle fought by the losing French forces at this famous battle.

At Waterloo, Napoleon fought his last (and losing) battle against an unbelievable number of enemies who all united to defeat him in this final battle that would shape Europe for generations to come. After Waterloo, Napoleon was exiled from France, and was later poisoned by his enemies. It was a sad and unfair ending to such a great man's life.

William stood perfectly still as he reviewed Tennyson's poem that was dedicated to Napoleon Bonaparte in his last days as the General and Leader of all of France.

THE CHARGE OF THE LIGHT BRIGADE

By Alfred Lord Tennyson
(presented in its original form)

1.
Half a league, half a league,
Half a league onward,
All in the valley of Death
Rode the six hundred.
"Forward, the Light Brigade.

Charge for the guns." he said:
Into the valley of Death
Rode the six hundred.

2.
"Forward, the Light Brigade."
Was there a man dismaye'd?
Not though the soldier knew
Someone had blundere'd:
Theirs not to make reply,
Theirs not to reason why,
Theirs but to do and die,
Into the valley of Death
Rode the six hundred.

3.
Cannon to right of them,
Cannon to left of them,
Cannon in front of them
Volleyed and thundere'd;
Stormed at with shot and shell,
Boldly they rode and well,
Into the jaws of Death,
Into the mouth of Hell
Rode the six hundred.

4.
Flashe'd all their sabres bare,
Flashe'd as they turned in air,
Sabring the gunners there,
Charging an army, while
  All the world wondere'd:
Plunged in the battery-smoke
Right through the line they broke;
Cossack and Russian

Reeled from the sabre stroke
  Shattered and sundered.
Then they rode back, but not
  Not the six hundred.

5.
Cannon to right of them,
Cannon to left of them,
Cannon behind them
  Volleyed and thundere'd;
Stormed at with shot and shell,
While horse and hero fell,
They that had fought so well
Came through the jaws of Death
Back from the mouth of Hell,
All that was left of them,
  Left of six hundred.

6.
When can their glory fade?
O the wild charge they made.
  All the world wondered.
Honour the charge they made.
Honour the Light Brigade,
  Noble six hundred.

MARIE ANTOINETTE

A WALK IN OLD PARIS

William snapped back to his present and looked around. He could see other landmarks in the distance that had withstood the ravages of time itself and stood there unchanged.

He was looking at two of the oldest and perhaps most beautiful of all the buildings. He was admiring the Grand Palace of the King and Queen, and of course, Notre Dame Cathedral where he had his little room. These two structures would go through very few changes in the faces that they put out to the world. And finally, just down the road a bit and in the distance, he could see the hulking and sinister-looking city prison called the Bastille.

William knew the complete history of the Bastille. It was the storming of the Bastille by the revolutionary mob in 1789 (thirteen years from the year he was now living in) that led to the French Revolution that ended up with Marie Antoinette losing her beautiful head.

He knew that the Bastille was torn down in later years, and an opera house was built in its place. He knew this because he had attended an opera there with his friend Margo when they had vacationed in Paris.

Yesterday, when he had walked this same route that he was following today, he had located where the Queen's racetrack was located. He had noted that the finer people of Paris began to arrive at the track in their beautiful horse-drawn carriages a little bit after noon.

It wasn't long after that before the royal carriage made its appearance. It was a very elegant-looking carriage, but the show-stopper was the Queen herself.

She was accompanied by an older man who was possibly in his middle thirties. This gentleman was dressed perfectly, and it was not hard for William to realize that he was looking at the "Darth Vader" or bad guy in this plot. It was the infamous Duc d'Orange. As interesting as the Duke was to William, it was the young Queen who stole the show.

She walked with the walk of a true queen, or perhaps even that of a true goddess from the ancient Greek world. Her eyes, which he could barely see from the distance, were cast with the brilliancy of emeralds. To look at her, one would only see an absolutely beautiful twenty-year-old woman who appeared to be full of sweetness and majesty.

She seemed to have the qualities that were needed to be a movie star back in William's time. The closest physical appearance that she easily brought to mind was a young Elizabeth Taylor, who was most famous for her role playing Cleopatra opposite the popular actor Richard Burton.

William's friend Josh from the University, was correct when he described her as outstandingly beautiful. She had light skin, yellow-blonde hair, and those emerald green eyes.

William's heart began to beat faster and faster as he thought about the plans he had made and the wonderful experience he was looking forward to with that fantastic body. It was no wonder that all the history books back home said that she was the talk of the European and French fashion world at this time.

She was wearing an extremely low-necked dress that showed off her well-developed bustline in all of its perfection. William was getting sweaty all over with the thought of having this exquisite woman, even if he had to share her with the evil Duc d'Orange. This assignment was getting more exciting and dangerous now that he could see two of the major players in the little drama that he was planning for tomorrow. He was eager to get on with it, and tomorrow could not get here soon enough for him!

He understood that the racing events went on for a total of three days, and that the Queen would be in attendance each day. Tomorrow was the final day, and Josh's history books told him that it was on the third and final day that the Queen would chose the lucky man to accompany her back to her bed at the local summer house where she stayed while she was in this part of Paris.

William watched from a distant vantage point as the races soon got under way. He stayed and watched everything until he felt comfortable that he knew the routine. Without anyone paying any attention to him, he was able to quietly slip away from the area as he continued his walk through the city.

He had decided to walk to the local shipping area which was down by the docks and watch the ships docking and pulling away. One ship in particular caught his eye, and he watched it being loaded with cargo. He watched with interest as the sunlight played across her tall sides while the ship swung heavily at her anchor.

Even at a far distance away from the ship, William could see the black tracery of her rigging and shrouds, the double line of her huge gunports, and the small scarlet rectangle made by her flags, flying the royal French colors as it flapped strongly in the freshening wind. The ship was a beautiful and exciting lady of the sea.

Often back home in Los Angeles, William and some of his friends would spend the day at the Long Beach Marina and watch the local ships and other vessels come in and out of their docking ports. Back home in the United States, and probably elsewhere in the world, raw materials and manufactured goods were sent into and out of the many world ports aboard shipping vessels such as the one he was watching now. The years may come and go, and the centuries along with them, but commerce by sea stays pretty much the same.

As he was turning away from the shipyard to continue his walk, he noted that the ship's riggings and sails were being unfurled, and her seventy-four gunports (he actually counted them on the side he could see and then doubled the count and added the usual four cannons across the rear of the ship, and the two usual ones at the front) were being opened and closed as if they were going through a process of getting oiled. She was probably getting ready to sail on the morning high tide when she would be full of provisions, gunpowder, cargo and men who gave their lives and love to the sea.

It was when he had walked about a block away from the port area, as he was retracing his steps back toward Notre Dame, that he was confronted with the huge body of a man who completely blocked his way.

JIM BOWIE, IF YOU PLEASE

A big smile crossed William's lips as he knew that he was about to find out if all the hours he had spent learning how to use Jim Bowie's "Toothpick" would pay off. He listened carefully to the man's hard-to-understand French, as he demanded William's money purse or his life. He told William that the choice was his, and it was said with a big smile upon his ugly face.

William Butler stood about six foot two in his stocking feet, and weighed about an even two hundred pounds of solid muscle. His opponent was a few inches shorter than he was, but he probably outweighed William by about thirty pounds. The match seemed even to William, and he slowly and carefully pulled his Bowie knife from out of its sheath, and slipped his right hand through the holding strap.

A small crowd had gathered around them, made up mostly of sailors and a few barmaids from the nearby taverns. Word travels fast when there was to be a fight in the streets, because everyone loves a good fight!

While the people formed a large circle around them, they both took off their rough-spun shirts and set them neatly aside.

William's opponent, who was being called "Roff" by the crowd of onlookers, looked big but flabby and possibly out of shape.

William, on the other hand, had the solid body of the bodybuilder that he used to be throughout his teenage years. William had always wanted to build up his personal muscular system while he was still growing and he succeeded. Since those early years, William had filled out well, and he stood there with Bowie knife in hand, looking like a young Brad Pitt when he was in great shape for his Hollywood movie *Troy*, where he played the part of Achilles, the greatest Greek hero to come out of the Trojan War.

The two grinning men started off slowly, circling each other as they went from left to right. They were both right-handed and basically around the same size. They were both holding their knives in a professional manner, with the thumb on top of the hilt, gripped by the rest of fingers so that the point was pointing outward.

Roff faked a straight lunge, ignored by William, who with a slashing motion caught a bit of Roffs hand as he was pulling it back. A red line became evident on Roff's knife hand as the two men continued moving.

William moved quickly to his left and saw that Roff was following his movement and also moved rapidly left. William put all his weight on his own left leg as he swept his right foot in a karate sweep behind the knees of his slower-moving opponent. Before he knew what was happening, Roff hit the ground, and the force of the landing knocked the knife out of his hand.

It was only a moment before William was sitting on the chest of the unarmed man, holding the sharp needle-point of his blade pointed at the eye of the now-frightened man.

"Yield or die, my man," said William in a voice that carried across the circle of onlookers. His English-tainted French was clearly understood by one and all. "And if you want to live, I suggest you yield and you say it right now."

"I yield! I yield! And I never even saw your move!"

A great roar went up from the crowd, and William made his knife disappear with a quick move, jumped to his feet and extended his right hand to Roff, who took it and allowed himself to be pulled to his feet.

William put his arm around the man and yelled to the crowd that the drinks were on him. William, with Roff in tow, led the shouting crowd into the nearest pub.

William was very pleased with how well his martial arts training worked on a real opponent. If he ever decided to stay in this time, he could put together quite a following!

What he really wanted to happen was that word would spread of the Englishman who quickly overcame a profession ruffian, and then bought him and the crowd drinks, as the new player in town. He knew that anything that had to do with men and fighting would definitely get back to the Queen, and that was just what he wanted.

William could have had his pick of the girls, and even though they were dirty, and not well-dressed, he had to force himself to pass on staying with one of them, and he was really sorry about that. There were also one or two others who caught his eye, but he needed to save his energy for tomorrow when he planned to meet the Queen, get rid of the Duc d'Orange, and have his way with Her Royal Highness.

THE QUEEN

It was not very difficult for William to gain entry into the royal racetrack. He had carefully dressed himself in his finest clothing, had hired a horse-drawn carriage, and had himself dropped off directly in front of the box office. A few small silver coins had paid his way into the fairly crowded area where he could see that the royal box was empty for the moment.

He had come early for the first race, knowing that Her Majesty usually arrived around the third race, and after making her presence known, would leave after the sixth or seventh race was completed.

William killed about an hour just walking around looking at all the nobility dressed in their finery. They really were most impressive and extremely polite, and he was deeply saddened when he thought that most of them would either be dead or in exile when the French Revolution finally arrived in the not-so-distant future.

Finally with the sound of the royal trumpets blowing, the Queen made her entrance.

William was thinking that if she was wonderful yesterday when he saw her from a great distance, she was utterly beyond words and beyond imagination when he was able to view her from a much closer location. Yesterday's colors were blue and a soft gray, but today's color was a soft silver-white that matched the powdered wig she was now wearing. She still had a low-cut bodice, and her breasts still looked inviting. Her hands and arms were allowed to show through, and the skin on them was a silky, smooth-looking, creamy white.

The royal party took only a few minutes to settle into their box seats, which looked down upon the entire encampment of people and racetrack. Standing in front of the stairs that led up to the royal box was one man whom William knew was the Queen's personal bodyguard, named Pierre.

Pierre had a bad reputation of being a man with a very short temper! It was said that he had killed or badly wounded more than twenty men, and the killing was always done with a sword, which seemed to be his choice of weapon.

William was pleased to find out that Pierre would not choose the knife over the sword, in that the sword was definitely William's own preference. Knives were only used very close up, and they could be sloppy, and usually both duelists came away injured.

William knew that the best thing to do was not to get involved with Pierre at all, but that did seem to be quite impossible if he was to make his move on the Queen. William realized that getting by Pierre was not going to be easy, and he could not think of any other way except to fight with him and probably get involved in a fight to the death. He could not see any other option to get rid of the man, and only a direct and frontal approach against him had any possibilities of success.

As always, his actions followed his thoughts, and minutes later, he was carefully working his way through the large crowd of people who were standing around in front of the royal box. This, of course, was the best place for them to see and be seen by everyone else. William was finally able to position himself into a position where only a single row of people stood between himself and the Royal Guard. Appearing to stumble, he plunged headlong into Pierre, who was knocked off his feet.

It was only a moment later that Pierre was back on his feet with his rapier in hand and pointing it at the as-yet-unarmed William, who tried to stand there with a confused look on his face. With an extremely and overly polite bow, William looked Pierre in the eye. "I beg your pardon, sir," William said with a large sweep of his hand in front of his body. "I believe you saved me from falling on my face in front of the Queen. It must have been her beauty that has transformed me into a clumsy bumpkin. It was so good of you to act as my bumper-stopper!"

"I acted as your *what?* What did you call me, you … you … Englishman?" Pierre finally finished sputtering and said in a clear and cold voice, "I demand satisfaction, and I demand it right now! Draw your sword, sir!"

William was pleased to see that all the noise they had created had gotten the attention of the Queen, who was looking directly down on them. He saw the hint of a smile on her beautiful face as he calmly drew his own rapier and faced the angry Pierre in an *en garde* position.

The people all around the two of them drew away and gave them plenty of room. There was hardly a sound as the two men glared at each other, while the surrounding crowd looked on and held its collective breath. Both men seemed to be about the same size and weight, and anyone looking at them would think that this should be an interesting duel. The crowd and the Queen, who continued looking down at the performance of the two men which was about to begin, all realized that this duel would be more exciting than just watching another horse race.

A complete hush came over the entire area as William had a moment to think to himself that all of the long months of training back in Los Angeles were finally coming down to these next few moments. The success of the mission would rise or fall based on his personal training and skill with the weapon. The man he was fighting was the product of a violent society, and Pierre was used to killing his opponent, as proved by his many kills, while he, William, had killed no one, fought to a draw with a girl on a baseball field, and had a lot of time put into practicing for this moment.

William was not feeling inferior in any way. He knew that he was the product of a superior society and that his instructor had taught him more moves than his opponent had ever thought of. All William had to do was to fight the way he was taught and not allow himself to feel any doubts or panic.

William looked across at Pierre, who appeared to be quite calm. It was obvious that Pierre knew his way around with a weapon in his hand. William watched him make a few moves to loosen up his muscles. He held himself as if it was an absolute certainty that he would make the kill, and that William was as good as dead.

They saluted each with their weapons, and the fight was on!

Pierre lunged swiftly, and William easily parried his blade. Pierre seemed surprised that William was able to block the thrust that he thought would end the contest before it really had begun. Pierre became a bit more cautious after discovering that William knew something about the weapon that he was holding in his right hand.

Pierre began to fence, working toward William and forcing him to defend himself in a backward moving defensive position. He was deliberately testing William to see just what he could do with a weapon in his hand.

William had the good sense to act clumsy, barely stopping some of the swift moves that Pierre was making. William was hoping that Pierre would underestimate his skill with a blade. This could only work to his advantage. William knew that he must hold back as he fended off Pierre's attacks, while watching for his own chance to have at him in his own way.

They were fighting with completely different styles. William continued to try and appear clumsy while defending himself with minimal skill.

Pierre was very strong! William could feel it in his strokes. Pierre also had the delicate touch of a master swordsman as he lunged again at William, who had to do a quick skip backward to save himself.

As it was, the tip of Pierre's blade ripped William's shirt and a gasp came from some onlookers, followed with whispered words of "Pierre is good, isn't he!"

Yes, Pierre was good. William discovered that quickly enough and was hard put to defend himself from the speed and skill of Pierre's attacks.

But the art of fencing had developed greatly from this time to William's twenty-first century. William knew things that Pierre would never even dream about, but the question that William was asking himself was whether or not he would survive long enough from Pierre's dancing blade for him to put them into play.

Sword blades were controlled largely with the fingers. The cuts were always made with the first few inches of the blade.

The whole idea was to make light, slicing cuts and not to try and overpower the opponent with large slashing moves.

William was able to see that his own defensive style was not familiar at all to Pierre, and he seemed to be somewhat disturbed by it. Pierre might be thinking that William was only lucky so far, and did not know just what it was that he was doing.

They fought savagely then, with all pretense thrown aside! It was thrust, parry, head fake back and forth. Pierre pressed hard, trying to end this duel that was going on too long for his liking. He was very intent now, ready to move in for the kill.

Every fencer tends to favor certain moves, those that are easy for him, to the exclusion of all others. A skillful man with a blade will soon determine which of these his opponent is likely to be unable to stop.

The crowd was closing in around them now. They sensed that the end was near. The Queen in her high perch was breathing heavily, paying strict attention to the life-and-death drama that was playing out just below her. She was enjoying every moment of it.

Pierre was smiling now, his eyes bright with purpose. He faked a head cut and then thrust at William's ribs.

William's defensive stroke was quick; he saw an opening in Pierre's defense but was too far away from him for a good body thrust, so with a flick of his wrist, William cut him along the inner sword arm with the back edge of his blade.

It sliced Pierre's arm deeply, and William saw him wince, saw him start to step back to prepare a defense, but he was too slow as William attacked instantly with a twenty-first-century-trained stroke. William faked left, then right, and Pierre was not familiar with what he was doing, and he was not fast enough to stop the direct thrust that went deep into his heart.

William pulled his blade back and watched as his would-be-killer slid silently to the ground. It had all happened very quickly.

William's breathing was fast and short, and he gasped to catch his breath. No one bothered him for a few moment, until one of the Queen's ladies-in-waiting came over and spoke to him for a few minutes.

William smiled and nodded his head. He was invited to attend an audience with Her Majesty at the big palace tomorrow for lunch. He looked up and received a golden smile and a nod from that beautiful face, and then the Queen was gone.

§

William was exhausted. He could hardly move. But he was happy! Everything had worked out well so far. He had the invitation he wanted, and he had just killed his first really bad guy. Things were looking up!

He walked slowly out the exit, heading for his waiting carriage to take him back to his room. Everyone respectfully made way for him, and the whispering behind his back began.

William did not look back at the body left lying there.

It didn't seem to matter what century men were in. Death, violence, love and lust, were the same no matter where the human race was. Some things never change, and William was not sure if that was a good thing or not.

VERSAILLES

An exhausted William had slept the entire night away, and awoke somewhat stiff but feeling surprisingly well. The muscles that he had used fighting the good fight with Pierre were those muscles that he normally used, so he had no real problems.

As soon as he did his usual morning workout exercises, he began to feel like himself again, and was ready to get on with what he hoped was his final day in Old Paris. He took the time to pull the Professor's worksheets on the Queen's residence, which was the royal palace of Versailles.

He wanted to read the Professor's points on the problems he might be coming across when he went to the palace later that afternoon.

Short note for William on Versailles by the professor:

Hello William Butler:

If you are reading these notes, which are intended for your eyes only after you have crashed the gate at the race, dealt with the probable personal bodyguard of the queen, and been invited back to the palace for a little fun and games, I congratulate you on your success so far, and I can't wait to get you back home so that I can take you out on the town, get you dead drunk, and squeeze out the exciting details from you.

Anyway, here is what you need to know about Versailles in case the duke or the queen bring up the subject.

Remember that any Frenchman or Englishman living in that time will have the following facts at their fingertips, so please put them into your memory.

§

The palace of Versailles is a royal château located in the countryside region of Paris, France. In French it is known as the Château de Versailles.

When the original château was built, the city of Versailles was just a small country village. In the timeline that you are now in, Versailles has become a very wealthy suburb of Paris. It is located about twenty miles south of the French capital in Paris.

The court of Versailles was the very center of political power in France after 1682, when King Louis XIV moved the center of his government to Versailles. About one hundred later, the royal court, threatened by the French revolution, moved back to the old capital, which of course was Paris. Since the royal family lived in and ruled the country from Versailles for over one hundred years, the location was not only known for its wonderful architecture, but as a symbol of absolute monarchy.

The earliest mention of Versailles that I could find in the French history books was dated as 1038, which means that the city was well known in France for over seven hundred years.

The official court was first established there on May 6, 1682. Several years later, after the upcoming French revolution, the buildings and grounds were turned into an art museum.

Napoleon Bonaparte, who was made the first emperor of France, moved his royal court into the palace at Versailles. His empress, Maria Louise, had her own apartments within the grounds. The emperor and empress were not getting along very well and lived in different parts of the large building.

I hope this brief sketch gives you enough to go on if the conversation goes in that direction. I am hoping to see you back home with all of us very soon.

Regards—the professor

VERSAILLES—CONTINUED

William took the special set of clothing out of his locked closet and went over all of the little pockets and places where he had secured knives, lockpicks, extra gold coins, and other emergency items. It was the Professor again who had insisted that he have all the backup items for a worse-case situation that might just come up unexpectedly.

William finally took his leave of the little room at the church for the last time. He knew that he would not be back, and he left behind everything that he did not need to have with him. The little room at the church had served its purpose well, and he never looked back at it as he headed over to the local bathhouse to clean himself up.

He was expected at the palace at one o'clock, which was the

posted time for the Queen's lunch. This gave him a lot of time to wash up, get trimmed, manicured, and garbed in his new French finery. It also gave him time for a late breakfast, which was coffee and some delightful French pastries.

At the appointed time of one o'clock, William Butler, citizen of the United States of America, a country which had not yet officially existed in this world of the year 1776, was led into the outside antechamber that connected to the dining room of the royal palace. The rooms that he passed through were definitively grand enough to put any other fancy room that he had ever been in to shame by comparison.

He came to a huge open chamber of gleaming gold and brass, stretching away in every direction for as far as the eye could comfortably see. The open view was broken up here and there, by many tall, intricately worked pillars of gold and silver. These pillars were set at regular intervals as much for effect as for anything else. The rooms were extremely impressive, but William expected nothing less. After all, this was the palace!

Heavily armed guards stood here and there, ostentatious in their shining silver armor and their visor-covered faces. No one ever paid them any attention. They were there to watch everything that was going on in the palace, and to ensure that peace and quiet would continue to happen within those majestic walls.

Just as William was getting quite bored standing around looking at the four walls, a side door opened and a tall, dark gentleman stepped into the room. William recognized the man as the Duc d'Orange, and felt terribly disappointed. He had been hoping that the third member of the expected trio would have been another woman. But instead here was the dangerous Duke himself.

The two men exchanged small talk and settled in on discussing William's duel with the bodyguard Pierre. The Duke told him that he was the talk of the palace and of the entire city of Paris. The Duke said that he was honored to personally meet "Sir William," and he thought that the Queen might ask him to stay on as her personal protector until she searched out someone new for the now-open position.

William was completely agreeable to everything the Duke had to say because it really didn't matter. William would either be very dead or very gone from the premises. The two of them finally ended up talking about the city of London, where William said he lived. This was a safe area for William to talk about because he had visited that wonderful old city at least five or six times and was the perfect tourist.

William said that he was now in Paris to meet up with several wine merchants to make arrangements to purchase next years' needs for his company back in England.

The Duke seemed satisfied with his cover story, and they moved on to talk about other things. They finally ended up talking about the young Queen and why William had really been invited to lunch.

The Duke was saying that Her Majesty had various sexual desires and fantasies, and that the two of them were lucky enough to try and help her achieve them. The Duke was very specific for William to get the general idea of what he, the new third party to the upcoming affair, had to do in the way of his duties and obligations to the Queen. The Duke spoke about everything in great detail, and the only item William thought he missed mentioning was the knife that he knew the Duke would be trying to put in his back during the extended orgy.

When the Duke was satisfied that William knew his complete role in the upcoming event, he made a significant little hand signal, and the doors leading into the ornate dining room were thrown wide open. The large dining-room table, which looked like it could sit at least thirty people, was set for two. The Duke said that the Queen had some affair of state that came up at the last moment, but she would be joining them after they had lunch. The Duke made the Queen's apologies which were gracefully accepted by William.

Knowing that they would not make an attempt on his life until they were all privately locked up in one of the bedrooms somewhere inside the vast palace, William did not hesitate to have a good lunch. It was not every day that he had the opportunity to sit down with a real duke in the palace of a queen, and be served lunch on the royal plates and use gold and silver knives and forks.

He went very easy on the wine, and only sipped at it after he saw the Duke drink his own wine from the same bottle.

MENAGE À TROIS

Her high heels clacked on the shiny marble floor as she entered the room. A soft glow emanated from inside the room as she stepped through the door.

She saw that there were candles all around that lit up the room. She was pleased at the special staging that the Duc d'Orange had set up for her. What she smiled at was the lovely living area, with a huge bed up against one of the far walls, and two comfortable-looking chairs on each side of the bed. Beyond the bed in the background was a large shaded window that overlooked the beautiful royal gardens.

She closed the door behind her and looked around to see if her chosen companions had arrived yet. Several vases of flowers adorned the room, and the smell of them filled the air. The queen was very pleased with the setting, and she would compliment the serving staff later. The "theatre" was set, and the "play-acting" would shortly begin.

She knew the script by heart, having played the same scene over and over with the duke and others. The duke and herself were the only returning players to their little play, and the excitement for her was usually discovering who the duke was going to bring in for the third player.

Usually the duke would pick some very pretty but poor peasant girl from one of the local villages. He would promise the girl several gold pieces, and the girl was always pleased to spend her afternoon alone with them.

It did not bother the queen at all that it was almost always a female as the third player, and that the duke spent an extra amount of time with the new girl and less time with her. The queen felt that she was being a good sport about sharing the duke with the other girl. And in all truth, she too enjoyed touching and fondling this other woman.

Every so often the duke would surprise her with a soldier from out of her very own royal army. When this happened, she would have a double dose of excitement. She would have the thrill of two males doing all those wonderful things to her body, and she would get to see the duke kill the unsuspecting man right in front of her very own eyes.

The soldier had to die, because they could not have him talking about what was going on with the queen. She understood all that, but what was so wonderful about being an eyewitness to a murder, was that the sex that followed with the duke, one on one, was more thrilling than anything else she had experienced in her young life, and she had experienced quite a bit already at the age of twenty.

Today was something that was different! Today, she had personally hand-picked the man to join them. It was that magnificent looking Englishman who had had that wonderful duel with her bodyguard Pierre. They had fought right in front of her raised box seat, and along with all the nobles who had come to the races, she was able to watch every exciting moment of that duel to the death. No one had ever come close to beating Pierre in a one-on-one contest of arms. That was why she had made him her personal protector. She wanted the best of the best!

When all of this was over, she would have to find a new bodyguard to protect her life and to provide her with night-time sex whenever the mood came upon her.

This Englishman, William something or other, had

accepted her lunch invitation, and she had remembered to tell the duke that, for this week, he did not have to find a stranger for them to act as a third party. She had already done that. She was always much happier when she knew who was coming, and this William person looked like a man who knew his way around.

The duel that had played out right in front of her box seat was so sexual and so stimulating, that she found that she was wetting herself. She had left right after the fight ended in order to go straight home and change her clothes and to daydream about today.

She knew that the duke would tell William what it was that was expected of him — and she always expected a lot! William would be good competition for the duke, who was beginning to get a bit too sure of himself around her. She might have to replace the duke with someone new, one of these days. A new man in her life was always exciting, at least for the first few times.

Here she was, sitting in their special soundproof room and running all of these things through her mind, when she heard the opening act of the play begin as the door opened.

THE FINAL ACT

She heard the duke's voice saying, "I've missed you, Marie. I've missed you so very, very much!" She smiled as she looked in his direction.

Another deep voice came from behind the duke. "I've missed you also, your majesty."

Both men crossed the room, and each sat down in one of the chairs that were facing her. She sat perfectly still on the end of the bed, smiling at them. Wonderfully hot flashes were beginning to whirl through her body as she sat there.

The duke moved in front of her, knelt down and took her hand in his. His brown eyes glittered in the soft candlelight, but it was the warmth of love shining from his face that completely melted her heart.

"Marie, I love you! I always have and I always will. I love having you in my life." His soft breath brushed across the back of her hand and he kissed it, sending tingles through her.

"Yes," she answered, hardly able to catch her breath. The duke stood up quickly and pulled her up and into his arms, where he kissed her softly on her waiting lips. He then released her to sit on the edge of the bed by herself once again.

To her surprise and pleasure, William took the duke's place, but he was on the other side of the bed as he went through the exact same words. Maybe it was because William was a new man in her life, or maybe he was just the better of the two men, but just soft and tender kiss really was something special. She felt herself beginning to get very excited!

Both men were now standing. They took off their outer clothing, and all that they were left wearing was tight-fitting black leather pants.

Earlier, when William was given the leather pants by the duke, it reminded him of Barbara Bennett and the sword fight on the baseball field back home. Barbara had come to his bed back in California wearing similar leathers and a great big smile. History often repeats itself in very strange ways, was his wandering thought.

The queen stood up, and she too removed her covering robe. Both men took in a deep breath as they looked at her standing there, proudly showing them her well-formed young, firm, twenty-year-old body. She was only wearing her high-heeled shoes, and a big smile. And the truth of the matter was that her smile was all that she really needed!

She knew that she was beautiful, and she put her own hands under each of her two breasts, and pushed them up and out toward them with the nipples hard and bright red in color. This was her own personal way of offering herself to the two of them.

William looked at the duke, who nodded, and they both went up to her, and each one took one of her arms and lifted her off of her feet. They placed her in the middle of the large bed and sat down beside her, one of them on each side of her. They were still holding on to her arms so that she could not move, while they each began to suck and fondle the large breast that was on their side.

The sensations now running through her body were unbelievable! She made a hopeless and half-hearted attempt to move, but had no real desire to resist. She was loving the double pleasure that she was receiving.

She felt herself beginning to burn up with internal heat, and she was hoping that would bring her to a climax soon because the pressure she was feeling internally was almost unbearable.

Each of the men took a long and slender thin piece of rope from the pocket of their leather pants. They then tied one end of the rope around her wrist, and the other to the headboard at the top of the bed. She was able to move her head from side to side, and her lower body was completely free, but that was all that was allowed to her.

The duke unfastened his leather pants and drew out his erection. As he stepped beside her at the side of the bed, she opened her mouth and took the full length of him into her mouth as she began to rock her head back and forth.

William saw that this was something that she must have done many times before. No one can take in that much without a gaging sensation taking over.

The queen had obviously overcome this problem with lots of practice, as she continued to rock her head back and forth. The look on the duke's face was one of complete pleasure.

William, in the meantime, had also removed his leather pants, and he too stood naked with an erection leading him. William was being very careful to always keep the duke in front of him where he was clearly able to watch him at all time. William knew that if he turned his back on him, a knife or a club to the head would be his reward for being stupid.

William saw that it was his turn to get into the action. The queen was still going strong with the duke, so he knew that the duke was not going anywhere soon. He positioned himself between her thrashing legs and entered her quite easily. She was obviously sexually stimulated, and she was very well lubricated, as he went in quickly and deeply.

The queen did not slow down her work upon the duke as William roughly banged away at her. William had no need to be gentle and he was in a personal great hurry to finish before the duke was done, so that he could continue to keep him in plain sight.

William had to admit that he was having a great time "sticking" it to the beautiful twenty-year-old queen. William finished up with a flurry and climbed down and went to one of the chairs, where he put his leather pants back on. He was not comfortable walking around naked.

William just sat there and watched the couple finish up. When he was done, the duke walked over to the other empty chair and put his pants back on.

The queen was still lying there trying to get her strength back. She was making soft sounds that William could not decide if it was pleasure or pain that she was expressing. He did not care either way.

The duke got up after his breathing had returned to normal and walked over to William. He told him that he had to take a bathroom break, and that he did not want the lady to cool down. While he was gone for a few minutes, he suggested that William continue to stroke her breasts to keep her going. The duke said that they were her most sensitive spots and that he knew that was where she liked to be touched the most.

The duke kept his eyes glued on William's back as William walked over and began to play with the generous breasts that were waiting upon his pleasure. Satisfied that William would be occupied for a few minutes, the duke turned his back on them and went out a side door which quietly closed behind him.

Quickly, William jumped off the bed. He took an extra moment and gave the other boob on the other side of the queen a little squeeze. William always liked to be an equal squeezer!

He carefully positioned himself on the side of the door that the duke had gone out of, so that when he returned, the duke would have to take one full step into the room before he could see the bed. What he would see was the wiggling figure of the woman, but no William. Before he could react to that, William would have his chance.

Long moments passed, and finally the door handle began to turn, and the duke took the first step into the room. He must have instantly sensed that something was wrong, because he had started to turn back toward the door when William pounced.

With all his weight and all his strength behind it, William threw his best right hook to the chin of the turning duke, who took the blow to his face straight on. He was unconscious before he started to fall to the floor.

A long-bladed knife that William knew was intended for his own back clattered down as the unconscious duke could hold it no longer. As the duke hit the floor, William took his head with one hand and his shoulders with the other, and he twisted with all of his might. A very satisfying 'crack' told that he had broken the neck of this evil man.

THE END IS NEAR

William checked for a heartbeat and found none. He also checked the duke's pulse and also found none. The duke was definitely a dead man.

William picked up the razor-sharp knife that the duke had dropped, studied it for a moment or two, and then threw it forcefully against the wall directly above the head board that still held the tied-up queen. He could see her trying to raise her head up so that she could see what was going on at the other side of the room.

William took a large handkerchief from out of his pocket, and walked over to the now-scared lady on the bed. Of course, she was expecting to see the duke, and was startled to see William walking around without that deadly knife protruding from his back.

William was going to stuff the handkerchief into her mouth. He did not want her to scream for help until he was finished doing a few things that needed to be done. Carefully, so as not to injure her mouth, which must have been tender from all the use it was getting from working over the duke, he pushed the gag in. He made absolutely sure that she was able to breathe out of her nose. He did not want to change the history of the world by killing off the queen of France before the French revolutionaries had at her. The thought of having her head cut off did not disturb him in the least. This was an evil woman.

In the back of his mind, he had another strange thought that needed to be discussed with the professor when he got home. What if a time traveler like himself, or someone else, decided to change history to make it more to their own personal liking? It seemed to William that doing something like this would not be a hard thing to do.

If Julius Caesar was protected from the "Ides of March" killing, and he did not die, would he have gone on to bring ancient Rome to further glory and perhaps made Rome the only true power in the world? That would have meant that his home world in the twenty-first century would have been part of the worldwide Roman city-state. There would have been no United States of America, no Europe as he knew it, and so on.

What if Abraham Lincoln's guard had stopped John Wilkes Booth from killing him that terrible night at the Ford theatre? Would the world with President Lincoln still in charge of the United States have been different than it was after the Civil War?

And speaking of the Civil War, what if the North's General Grant was taken out of the final days of big battles, and the South won the Civil War under General Robert E. Lee's leadership? Wouldn't the United States of America be a different place if the South had won?

What if someone went back and gave Alexander the Great the proper medicine so that he did not have to die at age thirty-four? Would the world not be different, because he then would not have had to divide up his conquests of the known world among his four surviving generals?

William knew that he could go on forever thinking about the "what ifs" of world history. Some of them would be good and others not so good, depending on who did what to whom. With his head spinning, he forced himself to take his wandering thoughts back to the problems he was now facing in the here and now.

William wanted something of the duke's and something of the Queen's to take back to Josh and the professor to prove that he had been here. He needed something to prove that he was with the queen, and that he had done all the things that he would be saying that he had done when he wrote up his adventures for the university's records.

He knew immediately just what he wanted to take back with him. From the duke, he took a pinkie ring that had the duke's initials and the royal crest of France engraved upon the largest emerald he had ever seen.

He walked over to the still-struggling queen and got on the bed next to her. He moved himself up and sat on her stomach while he removed a "simple" twelve-carat diamond necklace from around her beautiful neck.

At the time, when he had first looked at her when she stood there naked in front of the duke and himself, all he noticed that she was wearing, was the high-heeled shoes and a great big smile. Of course, she was also wearing this wonderful necklace, but he must have missed it because, like any normal guy, he was just looking at her boobs. He thought that this necklace would look better on one of his own special ladies who were waiting for him back home. It would be a lovely gift!

He also took three large diamond rings from her fingers. One for Josh, one for the professor and one for himself. After all, a little memory of this adventure was quite proper, in that tourists always brought things home with them.

He put the items carefully into his pants pocket and checked around the room to see if he had missed anything or if anything else needed his attention. The only thing that he could think of that needed to be done, was to give his "parting wishes" to the queen, but that could wait a few more minutes. He walked over to one of the chairs and sat down to review everything for one last time. He went over detail for detail upon all of the things, places and events that he had taken part of since he time-jumped into this time.

Once he left this scene permanently, he knew that someone, possibly a maid, would come to see why the queen had not reappeared. They would be in for a shock when they found the dearly departed Duc d'Orange, and Her Majesty the Queen lying there naked with her hands tied to the bed's headboard.

William grinned to himself as he saw the strange scene unfold in his imagination. Naturally, everything would be covered up since this was the queen of France, and she would continue on with her evil ways until her subjects found their own special way of dealing with her and the rest of the royal family.

William stood up and looked around the room one last time. He thought that he had gathered up all the materials that he needed to take back with him in order to complete the history department's project. He would probably take a year off to relax and take a well-deserved vacation. His biggest problem was, which of his special girls in Los Angeles should he take with him on his well-earned vacation? Right now he had his fill of the time-travel thing, and he was quite pleased knowing that he had handled this assignment well.

The last thing left to do was to untie the queen and give her his last and best parting shot.

William gently unbound her raw wrists from the ropes that held them in place. He never spoke a word as he took the gag out of her mouth so that she could breathe freely once again. He then turned the queen over on her hands and knees.

He entered her once more, only this time he went slowly and carefully. He reached forward and played with her beautiful breasts for the last time. He really would miss them. He was definitely a breast man, and the queen had one of the finest sets he had ever been allowed to touch.

He continued to pump into this woman, going deeper and deeper until he was in as far as he could go. Minutes later he was done and he got off the exhausted woman and pulled up his black leather pants.

He stood perfectly still and willed himself back to the starting point of the entire adventure in the twenty-first century. He was going home!

ABOUT THE AUTHOR

WHO IS THE REAL BUD SELIGSON?

Bud Seligson, who was born in Chicago, Illinois, has been a ghostwriter to many of the major well-known writers of today's fiction and science fiction. He is also well known in Hollywood as a "story doctor" for many studios. Bud lives in Los Angeles with his wife, Diane, who is his co-writer and sometime editor.

www.ingramcontent.com/pod-product-compliance
Lightning Source LLC
Chambersburg PA
CBHW020641250626
47154CB00008B/2768